HER
MONSTER

HER MONSTER

A NOVEL

JEFF COLLIGNON

08613557

Copyright © 1992 by Jeff Collignon
All rights reserved.
Published by
Soho Press Inc.
853 Broadway
New York, NY 10003

Library of Congress Cataloging-in-Publication Data
Collignon, Jeff, 1953-
Her monster / by Jeff Collignon.
p. cm.
ISBN 1-56947-001-4
I. Title.
PS3553.C474673H47 1992   91-44363
813'.54—dc20   CIP
                  r91

Manufactured in the United States
10   9   8   7   6   5   4   3   2

Book design and composition by
The Sarabande Press

Teratology
The study of the production, development,
classification and anatomy
of monsters.

HER
MONSTER

CHAPTER

1

"**EDWARD,**" the old woman calls.

"Fuck you," I answer.

"Edward, don't be that way."

"What way?" I ask innocently, glancing at the door.

From the other side of the door, she responds, "The way you're being. Can't you just let things go, let them be the way they are."

At this, I give a short barking laugh. Old age has made her simple. "How can I let them be any other way, you old fool."

"You don't have to be so unkind."

"I can if I want to."

"But why would you want to?"

The conversation is absurd. I see no need to continue it.

"Did you bring the stuff?" I ask, changing the subject to safer ground.

"Yes."

"Why don't you just leave it on the doorstep. I'll get it in a little while."

"Can't I see you?"

"Why?"

"Why," she repeats slowly, as if not quite understanding the word.

"Yeah, why?"

"Because I love you and I want to know that you're all right."

"I'm just hunky-dory, and I'm really happy that you love me. Now leave the stuff and go away, okay?"

"Edward," she wails, starting the whole thing all over again. Seeing no need for a change in dialogue, I answer, "Fuck you."

Ten minutes pass and she leaves. I stand by the window peering out from the side. Once I'm sure she's gone, I open the door and pick up the three shopping bags she has left.

In two of them are canned goods, six chickens, five loaves of bread, four six-packs of beer, two cartons of cigarettes, and three packages of Oreo cookies. I attack the cookies, stuffing three of them into my mouth.

Chewing and drooling black saliva, I dive into the last bag. Inside are books. I examine each of the books carefully, having little faith in her ability to follow instructions. She has surprised me this time: each is one that I had ordered.

I stuff two more cookies into my mouth, and drool all over my chest as I put away the groceries. The books I place on top of my desk. Then, swallowing hugely, I light up a cigarette. An unfiltered Camel.

I draw the smoke deep into my rasping lungs and hold it for as long as I can, before expelling it all in one rasp. The acrid smoke mingles nicely with the sweetness of the cookies. I do it again, and then again and again, until the cigarette stub threatens to burn my fingers. I crush it out on the wood floor, using the callused pad of my right foot. The smeared butt fits in nicely with all the others strewn across the wooden floor. I glance around the front room of my cabin, seeing the debris of my life and am not at all bothered by it. It may not be to everyone's taste, but to mine it seems just fine.

I pop a beer and carry the can outside to the front porch. As always, the silence surrounds me. It continually surprises me how quiet it is here, though after eight years I would have thought it would no longer have that effect. A complete absence of sound. No bird or insect comes near my cabin. They fear me, it would seem, as much as everyone else does.

"Assholes," I mutter disgustedly, then hunch down, resting on the heels of my feet. My toes crab into the wood, clawing ten indentations into the planks. I flex the muscles of my toes, feeling the wood give and begin to splinter. I relax and glance down at the score of claw marks and tears in the porch. If I'm not careful, I'm going to end up having to completely rebuild the porch. A project I would not enjoy. I'm too clumsy to even attempt something like that. I've never had that ability. I like to think it's the weird configuration of my body that precludes this, but deep down I know it's only because I'm such an oaf. Coordination is not one of my attributes, at least coordination in the normal pursuits of a human life. My existence is not dictated by these parameters. In the chase, I am unequaled. I move with a speed and power that no Olympian could ever duplicate. Of course there are other drawbacks to this. One being that I can only run with mouth agape and both arms twisted behind me, held straight up in the air. I have been told, by one who supposedly cares for me, that I look like some huge bird of prey descending on his victim. It's a description that never inspired in me a great desire to race.

I retreat into the cabin for another Oreo and cigarette. Chewing and smoking, I hunch down again, leaning the knobs of my spine against the wall. My toes claw a secure foothold and I lean back, smoking, chewing, and drooling. For the moment, I am perfectly content.

The cabin sits twelve miles from the nearest town. The last mile and a half can only be negotiated on foot. It's treacherous and can only be managed by someone who knows the way. The old woman knows the path well. That she seems to have kept that knowledge to herself, surprises me. She's such a garrulous old fool, I never would have thought she had it in her. It's nice occasionally to be surprised by people.

The cabin is surrounded by forest. I have no idea who actually built the place, and have often wondered if maybe it wasn't someone like me. The old woman says Morton Holdridge owned it before me. That's all she says. She's never researched it any further than that. She isn't the type to look at anything too closely and accepts everything at face value. If there's any doubt of that, there's me as prima facie evidence.

Still, I wonder about Holdridge. Who was he? Did he actually build the place? The cabin is so inaccessible that only a freak like me, or someone well beyond the dimensions of normal misanthropy, would ever consider living here. Which was Holdridge, I wonder? Did he also sit here and look out? And if he did, what did he see? The beauty of the woods, the silence of the land? Or did he see it all as a spacious prison, intended to hold a single inmate?

I take a drag off my cigarette and glance down at it, noticing a smear of red on the white tip. I touch my lip gently. My fingers come away smudged with crimson. I've been gnashing my teeth again. It's a habit I can't seem to break. Living alone makes it difficult to identify bad habits. There's no one around to point them out. I wipe my arm across my mouth, examining the red smear. It always surprises me to see my own blood. I always expect it to be a different color. Everything else about me is so different. Why shouldn't my blood be, too?

The doctor who delivered me was also surprised by this. I remember the old woman telling me about his astonishment that anything that looked like me could bleed the same fluids as a human being. It amazed him. He wanted to write a paper about it, he wanted to be famous. All he became was dead. He took the secret of my birth with him, leaving it to the three of us. Though we went our separate ways, from that day forward we were inextricably bound. The old woman, the old man, and I. What times we had.

The sun begins to touch the top of the trees and I can feel the air beginning to chill. I rise, face the sunset, and watch it slowly begin to die. As its blood shoots across the horizon, staining everything in a carnelian hue, I lift my head and howl, letting my voice echo through the woods, feeling it burst from my chest in one glorious scream.

Late evening and I sit before the stove, paging through my new books. The kerosene lamp flickers, casting monstrous shadows against the walls.

At the back of my new *American Heritage Dictionary,* I find a letter pressed between the pages. I pick it up, examining it closely, annoyed that the old woman hadn't told me it was there. It could have languished there forever if I hadn't decided to page through the book.

It's addressed to Eddie Talbot, and the return address is the John Crawford Literary Agency Ltd, New York.

"Dear Eddie," it begins, and I smile, feeling my incisors press against my lower lip.

Congratulations on the new book. Daw loves it as they have all the others, but for this next one they want something more. They want a love interest for Alovar. They seem to feel (and I agree with them) that you're losing a large percentage of your audience by refusing to introduce Alovar to any feminine character. It doesn't have to be a great love affair. But for God's sake, can't you let the guy get laid occasionally? They think it would mean a big boost in sales.

Think about it and see what you can do.

Sincerely,
John

I reread the letter, stick it back in the Z section, and begin to pace. Movement seems to help. It burns away some of my anger, but what it leaves in its place is the ash of depression.

How can I write about women? What do I know about women? I know they are pretty to look at, but beyond that, what woman do I know? Only the old one. And I doubt that she is the template for femininity. Could she possibly be Alovar's "love interest," with her sagging breasts and heavy thighs? Is this what my Warrior of the Wasteland is doomed to woo and conquer? The thought disgusts me, but she is the only woman I know, the only one I have ever conversed with.

I pause at the window; looking out I see only my own reflection. What woman, I wonder, would ever want to talk to something like that? And if she did, would this be a woman I would even want to talk to? Some bizarre, fetish-ridden hag, who might think it would be interesting to bed a monster.

The hair on the back of my shoulders begins to quiver and stand on end. I feel the anger biting into me. I try to control it, but it's too fast, too brutal to turn aside. I feel the howl beginning in my chest. It explodes from my jaws, echoing around the room, and I rush outside into the night, screaming at the waning moon. My arms lift behind, reaching into the night sky, and with my jaws agape, chewing the wind, I dart into the forest. Crouching low to the ground, my feet claw at the earth, pushing it behind me until it seems that I am moving on a curtain of air, swiftly navigating around trees and bursting through bushes. The howl echoes behind me, crashing off the trunks of trees and bouncing back and forth until it seems to scream only inside of my own head.

This sudden burst of energy leaves me on all fours panting for breath. Saliva drools from my jaws onto the ground. I inhale deeply, picking up the old scent of rabbit and squirrel. My toes and fingers dig into the earth, planting themselves, and from their root blooms me, some grotesque parody of a biped. A twisted joke of a being.

I lower my head to the ground. My nostrils quiver, snuffing the earth, and for a moment, in my exhaustion, I find peace.

Standing before the typewriter, I begin to work on Alovar. It will be my fifth book in the series. Before Alovar there were two other books in the science fiction genre, each with different characters. When I had first discovered Alovar, I thought he would soon pass as the others had, but something about him drove me to continue him through three other books. Now I am as tied to Alovar as he is to me.

I let the typewriter draw me in and soon I am with my warrior. . . .

Alovar, exiled to the wastelands by the sheer perfection of his form, wandered the ravaged lands, helping those he could and showing mercy to those he couldn't. He never questioned the decree condemning him to this existence, for Alovar was a warrior, a man whose code forbid the faintest hint of equivocation. While the terms of his life were his own, the path his life took would be ordained, as were all men's paths, by a higher force. Alovar knew there was wisdom in this, a wisdom that he, as a mere mortal, could never hope to understand. It was enough to be directed. He felt honored that the gods had bestowed this harsh test upon him.

The land had worked its way into him until soon it was as if Alovar had never known any other existence. The time of banquets and royal festivals was long past. The mutants, the scorched earth, and the lost lands were now Alovar's only world. The sheer depravity in this new civilization no longer had the capacity to either surprise or shock Alovar, because he had become a part of it now. He had become as barbaric as those he fought and as compassionate as those he defended. He had become the dream made real. The warrior who suddenly appeared as if from nowhere, and then after accomplishing his goal would disappear into that same fabric. He was the forgotten consciousness of a people so buffeted and abused that they had no time for memory. Alovar became that memory.

Many, seeing him move along the land, would be haunted by vague memories of times past. The memories would never quite bloom to fruition, but they would instigate small acts of kindness, a sentiment so long forgotten that they would surprise both the recipient and the donor of these benefices.

Locked within his code of honor, Alovar traveled from one end of the wastelands to the other. His sword was always honed to razor sharpness and kept close to hand.

In the northeast, in his travels, he came across a small band of Marauders abusing and torturing a battered group of mutants.

Hidden behind the trunk of a gnarled and dying tree, Alovar watched the cruelty until he could stand it no longer. He rushed across the sand, his sword glinting in the murky light, and fell upon the Marauders. He moved among them like a whirlwind of doom. His sword flashed, cutting and thrusting into the bellies of the offenders, until only one still stood. A huge man. Marred by old battle scars, he paused and stared in astonishment at Alovar's perfect form.

"I've heard tell of you, pretty one," the Marauder sneered, recovering from the sight of this handsome avenger. "When I'm done with you, I shall have you as my boy, and you will learn of pleasure beyond anything you have ever known."

Alovar stared without expression at this creature standing before him. He took in the man's unkempt appearance, and the cruel twist of his lips, and he raised his sword.

"You'll not speak to me now, my pretty one, but soon you'll call out in desire for my pleasure," the Barbarian cooed.

Alovar crouched and waited.

The Barbarian rushed, feinting towards Alovar's head. Alovar ignored the feint and quickly brought his sword to bear against the other's attack towards his belly. Using his great strength, he swung his sword in a full circle, carrying the Barbarian's thrust up into the air. Stepping back suddenly, leaving the Barbarian momentarily off balance, Alovar thrust forward into the other's entrails.

The Barbarian grunted and staggered back, pulling himself off the point of the sword. His hand slapped at his wound in a futile attempt to staunch the blood. "Pretty one," he grunted, spewing blood across his lips, then fell to the ground.

Alovar impassively wiped the edge of his sword, then thrust it back into its golden scabbard.

"Why do you do this?"

Alovar turned at the sound of the voice to see one of the mutants standing before him. He examined the man, noting the extra flap of flesh covering his eyes and the seven fingers at the end of each hand.

"Why, why do you do this thing? For what purpose?" the mutant asked, then turned and gestured to the group of men and women standing behind him. "Do you want one of us for your pleasure?"

Alovar studied the man for a moment, then glanced at the rest of the group. The spokesman was the least deformed. The others were a tangle of extra limbs and horny flesh. The women, he noticed, were by far the worst, but in this time of disease and famine any woman was highly prized.

Alovar ignored the man's question and stepped up to one of the woman. She cowered before him, hiding her face behind one hand that lacked fingers, and another that carried only thumbs.

"For this," Alovar said, resting his hand against the swollen mound of the woman's belly.

"You want the baby?" the spokesman asked calmly, seemingly unsurprised by this request.

Alovar's quick glance of disgust shamed the man. And in his shame, he suddenly understood that this was not a man who fought for reward, but a man who fought for only virtue. It was a concept that seemed foreign to him, but one that also seemed to stir vague memories within his mind.

The woman tentatively brought her hand down to rest against Alovar's. Her eyes slowly crawled up across his chest to catch his.

For a moment Alovar was aware of only the nascent being in the woman's hard belly and the depth of her gaze.

"It is all right, little mother. All shall be well for you and your child," Alovar said, then suddenly smiled. His smile was like a golden light that shone upon the woman. She bathed in it, and wished that it would never leave her.

Her fingerless hand pressed more tightly against his, trying to press the warmth of his palm deep into her belly, into the life that grew there. For a moment she could almost feel the strength of him seeping into herself, and it was a strength that she welcomed for she had known only fear and weakness for too long.

"It will be good," Alovar told her, then gently pulled his hand from her grip.

The woman felt the coldness form around the place his hand had been. She longed for a return of his hand, but was suddenly surprised by a movement within her belly, a warm surge of strength that filled both her and her child. Her face twisted into a smile, an awkward gesture that she had long since forgotten how to make.

Seeing the attempted smile, Alovar bowed to her, then turned and began to stride across the desert floor.

"What do they call you?" the spokesman cried out, as Alovar crested a hill.

Against the sunlight, Alovar turned to look down at the small group of men and women, and raising his arm high into the air, replied, "Only a man," then turned and disappeared from sight.

CHAPTER

2

ANOTHER CHECK CAME in the mail today. I don't understand it. Why would they give him so much money for those awful stories he writes? It makes a body wonder just what kind of people live out there in the cities. Already we have more money from his books than Ted and I ever had from all those years he worked at the plant. I just don't understand how money got to be so cheap.

I'm tired tonight. I walked all the way up there and again he wouldn't even step outside to say hello to me. It's been almost a year now since I've seen him. I wonder how he looks. He'd never let me take any pictures of him, so I don't even have that to remember him by. Wonder if he's taking care of himself. He sure drinks a lot of beer, and those cigarettes he smokes are going to be the death of him.

Mr. Dykes came over last night with the books. Don't know what I'd do without that man. He's been so kind and helpful and hasn't been at all pushy about things, though there've been times when I wished he would be a little. He makes me feel all girlish again, which at my age is no easy matter. But there's something about him that just makes me all weak and silly when I see him. Maybe it's those blue eyes of his. They always seem to be smiling, as if he doesn't have a care in the world. It's nice to be around someone who doesn't have worries. Lord knows, I have enough for both of us.

What with all my trying to get Eddie to come out and talk to me, I forgot all about the letter. I hope he finds it. Don't know if it's important. Doesn't seem like they ever are, but I guess there's always a first time. I'll have to remind myself to mention it to him next week.

Marilyn called a little while ago, wanted to know if I was going to help out at the church tomorrow morning. I told her, just like I always tell her—but Marilyn never seems to listen—that I just don't have that kind of feeling anymore. She went right on, talking about all the stuff they had to do for Pastor John, never paying the least bit of attention to what I'd said. It wasn't another ten minutes or so before she asked me what time was I going to be there. Then I told her again. "Marilyn," I said, "I've lost that religion feeling. I sure wish it'd come back, but there's no forcing something if it isn't there anymore."

That shut her up for a minute or two, but not for too long. Hard to get the last word in on Marilyn. She came right back with how God's patient and wants all of us to find our own way to him, no matter how far astray we've gone. She told me, what I needed to do was just get down on my knees and pray, and God would come right back to me and show me the way. I didn't say anything. I didn't tell her about the last time I asked for God to do just that. I figured if I did, I'd end up talking all about the family—things that we'd sworn to never talk about, with anybody. I let her talk on and told her I would sure try.

It's not so hard now not talking with anybody about Eddie. After Ted died, God rest his soul (though I don't know if God's going to have too much to do with Ted after what he did and all), I was pretty near crazy trying to figure things out. All those people coming around the house, looking in every nook and cranny. Seemed like it was only a matter of time before someone happened to go up into the attic. I don't know what I would have done if they had. I know what Eddie said he'd do, and it near broke my heart hearing him come out with those words. Him being barely seventeen years old and saying he had nothing left to live for. I knew right then I had to do something. It was Eddie that finally told me what we should do. It surprised me that he knew so much about those things. I guess he got it from all the books. He was always reading. Don't know where that came from. Ted never read anything, unless you count the sports page and the funnies, and I never had much use for it myself, but that boy seem to be reading from the first day he could walk. I remember that first time I found him sprawled across the floor of the attic with that magazine all crumpled up in his face. He wasn't much more than a baby, sniffing and snorting at it, like he didn't know if it was for eating or reading.

"What is this?" he asked, with his face all scrunched up like it gets when he doesn't understand something.

"A magazine," I told him, still not knowing what he had.

"What's all these wormy things?" he asked, and that's when I walked over to see just what he had gotten a hold of. Well, let me tell you, I don't know where that magazine came from. Ted never had no use for them. Only thing I can think of is the people who used to own the house must have kept them hidden up there. I looked down at that boy, and there he was with his nose pressed right into that naked woman's stomach, sniffing and snorting like it was something more than a picture.

"What'd you think you're doing?" I said, reaching down

nd snatching that magazine out of his hands. And before he even knew what was happening, I cracked him right across the forehead with it. I was so mad I didn't even think about what I was doing. Seemed to me it was bad enough he was the way he was, but being a pervert on top of it was just going to make everything a whole lot worse. Eddie, he just looked up at me, his face all scrunched, and those big brown eyes of his started leaking the biggest tears I'd ever seen. It seems to me, that was the last time I ever saw Eddie cry. Boy couldn't have been more than four or five. Hard to think of a kid having his last cry at four. Seems like crying might be a good thing for a child, but then I guess Eddie's never really been one. He's always been something else.

I started him on reading then. Seemed like he took to it like a house on fire. Soon I couldn't give him enough books. He read everything at least twice. Sometimes he'd want to talk about it. I remember once he'd read some books written by a Frenchman, and he started asking me all about life and was life anything more than just a whole lot of moments all strung together. I remember that, because it seemed like a mighty depressing way of looking at things. I tried to tell him that life was a path that led up a mountain to the true glory of God. (This was before all the trouble started with Ted.) Eddie didn't say anything to that, though I could tell he didn't agree with me. He'd always been a good boy, despite everything else about him. He just nodded and went back to his book. But there's something else I recall about that day. I was leaving, and right before I unhooked the ladder, letting me down from the attic, Eddie, he looked over at me with those big eyes of his and those teeth jutting out from his lips, and he said, "But, Mom, if I can't get through the moment, how can I ever find the path that's going to take me up the mountain?"

It gave me pause. He was five and a half. "God'll show yc the way," I told him, never doubting it for a moment.

"Nobody knows I'm up here," he said. "How's God going to find me in the attic?"

I told him God always knew where he was, then I went downstairs, smiling to myself, thinking about how cute it was that Eddie didn't understand about God. Later, after all the trouble with Ted, I began to think that maybe Eddie was right, maybe God just never looked in attics for people, maybe he never realized just how hard things can be for some folks. Seems like some he just makes and puts out in the world, like a Chevrolet or something, and never thinks about them no more.

It was Eddie who came up with the idea to move. He's the one who said it wasn't no good anymore—trying to hide everything, the way we were. He told me what we should buy and how we should do it. Sure surprised me, some of the things he knew: about the insurance, about selling the house, and even how to go about finding this cabin we got for him up in the woods. 'Course by then he'd just sold that first book of his to those New York people. It sure stunned me when he told me about that. I knew he was writing up there, but it never occurred to me he was writing books. Seemed like it was mighty stupid of me now not to know that, what with the typewriter he asked for and all that paper, but it just never occurred to me somehow that he could do that. What kind of a mind has all those words inside it just fighting and busting to get out. Not anybody from my side of the family was ever anything like that, and I know Ted's side had only a few words in their whole family, and a couple of those they wouldn't even let out through their mouths let alone put on a piece of paper.

I remember bringing that letter up to Eddie and the way

he opened it, so delicate like with those big clawed hands of his. How he bowed over it, and the way the hair on his shoulders and neck started quivering.

"What's wrong?" I asked him, thinking like a fool he'd gotten some bad news. Why, there wasn't anybody he knew that could give him bad news, except me. I was the only person alive anymore that even knew he was there.

"They bought my book," Eddie said, looking up at me, his teeth bared in what passed for a grin.

"What're you talking about, boy?" I said.

"My book. I wrote it and they're giving me money for it." Eddie said, sounding strong in a way I'd never heard before.

"You wrote a book?" I said.

"Yes, and this is the money they're giving me for it," he answered, holding out a piece of paper to me. "And there's going to be more. This is only the first check."

I took the paper from him and, sure enough, written right across the top of it, was the name Edward Talbot, and below that was a figure that seemed to have more zeroes than I'd ever seen before.

"But what . . . ," I started, and then couldn't think of anything else to say.

"It's a book, Mom. It's what I've been doing up here all these years. It's only the first one, and there's going to be more and there's going to be money coming in on a regular basis."

"What'd you write about?" I asked, suddenly fearful. "You didn't write anything—"

Eddie shook his shaggy head. No, he hadn't wrote anything about that. He said the book was about the future and what he thought the future was going to be like. I could tell the boy was pleased about it, and I figured if they were giving him money for it, then he had to know what he was doing.

"What's it called?" I asked, not being able to stop the smile that started on my face, knowing it for one of pride over my son's talents, trying to remember if I'd ever been able to smile that way before.

"It's called *The Abomination*," Eddie said, looking right at me until I couldn't stand it anymore and glanced away, remembering the last time we'd heard that word, Ted coming up the attic stairs with the ax, screaming that one word over and over again.

"Oh Eddie," I said, moving towards him, holding my arms out to him. And he came to me that time. I think that might've been the last I got to hold him, and I got to say no matter how strange he may look, or how odd his body appears to be, he fit just perfectly in my arms.

He finally pushed back a bit, then, still holding on to me, he started to tell me what we were going to do.

"But there's not enough money here." I told him.

"There's going to be more coming in, and with his insurance money we can do it."

I'd never heard him call Ted anything else: never Dad, Father, or even Ted. It was always *he,* never anything more than that.

Maybe he could smell it on him, could smell that scent of deceit and corruption.

I bought a van with dark tinted windows, and we set out two weeks later for Idaho. That was a happy time for us, traveling across the country, Eddie like a two-year-old in the back, peering out the window, constantly asking me about things. What was that? And did that smell like this? And was this a hard or a soft thing? We drove clear across the country that way, and there was a part of me that never wanted that trip to end.

Some nights, instead of even pulling up to a motel, I'd just sleep right in the back with Eddie. I'd fall asleep, listening to the sound of his rasping breath. Sometimes, if we'd found a secluded place somewhere, Eddie'd get to come outside. And watching him then, I'd always think of that time I saw a newborn colt try its legs out for the first time, staggering around, staring out at everything with its big eyes, until its legs started to straighten up, and then in no time at all it was racing around the corral, prancing and kicking the air. That's what it was like for Eddie. It was still a corral, but it was a bigger one than he'd ever known before.

When we finally came up into Idaho, I was a little disappointed to have the trip come to an end. I could tell Eddie was, too, but he never said nothing about it. I think we both knew that it had to end, that we couldn't just keep driving around forever, as nice as it would have been.

It took us another week before we found the cabin. Eddie took right to cabin living. Seemed like that first week when I was up there trying to help him, he'd get annoyed with me whenever I did anything. Took me a while to understand that this was his place, that he didn't want his mama making it into something else. Once I understood that, I started leaving him alone and just sat back and watched.

He did a good job on it. He turned it into a comfortable place, at least comfortable for him. Didn't have no chairs, because Eddie's never been able to sit down real well. That hump running down his back makes it almost impossible for him to do that. He's only comfortable standing or lying down on his side, anything else stiffens him up, he says, and looking at his body I can understand why that would be.

After a few days he tried to send me away, said it was time I went and started putting my own place together. I think he could tell I was afraid, and knew that if he didn't push me out I'd never leave. I sure didn't want to. It'd been almost twenty-one years since I'd been on my own without a man around the house, and suddenly thinking about it made me awfully nervous.

"You can visit me whenever you want, Mother," Eddie told me.

"Awful long way to come for a visit," I said. "Maybe it'd be better if I just stayed here."

"Then who'd bring up the supplies?" Eddie asked patiently, knowing what I was doing and trying not to be too hard on me.

"I could just go down to get them every week or so."

"People'd start to talk, start to wonder where you lived and what you were doing up here all by yourself. No time at all they'd come up to visit, see how you were doing."

"What'd be wrong with that?" I asked, without even thinking about it.

Eddie didn't answer for a moment, and when he did he turned away and looked out the window towards the forest. "Then I'd be back in another attic," he said softly.

"It wouldn't have to be that way," I said, knowing full well I wasn't thinking about anybody but myself.

Eddie turned to look at me, then glanced away and said, "No, I guess it wouldn't. You want to stay, you stay." He stepped outside onto the porch.

I stood in the middle of that room, looking around, thinking where I'd put my chair, and how I could sit up late at night by the cook stove, listening to the sound of my son's typewriter up above me in the attic, when it occurred to me that there wasn't any attic, there was just a fruit cellar dug down below the floor boards of the kitchen. I found myself thinking that it wouldn't be too bad. I'd still be able to hear that typewriter, when I suddenly caught myself. I was thinking of putting my son into a hole in the ground just because I was a little afraid of living on my own.

I went outside. Eddie was standing on the porch with his head thrust back, snuffing the air as if he was taking in all those clean smells as if for the last time.

"I'll just stay the night, then go into town in the morning."

"It's okay, Mother. You want to stay, it's okay with me," Eddie said without turning, still looking out towards the forest.

"No, I need to be on my own for a while." I touched his arm, feeling the warmth of him beneath the coarse hair. "I think maybe we all need to do that for a while."

That's when he turned and looked at me, and a moment later bared his teeth into a grin.

"Well then, why don't I cook you dinner tonight," Eddie said. "But first, I've got a little surprise for you."

In a flash, he darted off the porch steps and around the cabin. He came around the other end, howling with excitement, and in his hands was the most rickety piece of a chair I'd ever seen in my life. But Eddie, he carried it like it was a throne. He put it right in the center of the room and made me sit down in it, said it was mine, said whenever I came to visit that chair would always be waiting for me. Couple of months ago when I went out there with supplies, I saw that chair down by the side of his cabin all broken up, with claw marks across the side of it.

Things didn't get bad right off. For a while Eddie was always outside waiting for me. Seemed like we both had lots of things to tell each other, but over the years those times became less and less. It got so as I was just like a mailman to Eddie. He always asked for the mail first, and then maybe he'd ask how I was doing. 'Course there was things going on in my own life. I'd made some friends, and a few of the local widowers had started calling around the house, and a couple of them seemed like very nice gentlemen.

I'm not ashamed to admit to going out with more than a few of them. But I always let them know right off that I wasn't interested in anything serious, and it seemed like once that was understood, we just set out to have a good time. And we did have some good times, times I don't ever remember having with Ted. 'Course I never forgot about Eddie. I always showed up with his supplies. Maybe I was late a few times, but I always did get there.

That one time, a couple of years ago, wasn't any fault of my own. There was a heavy snowfall, and I think it was Tommy that I was seeing at that time, Tommy convinced me I shouldn't try any kind of trip anywhere with the way the weather'd been. It was so cozy lying up with him, that I just didn't have the heart to get all bundled and make that trip into the mountains. I got up there a week or two late, but I made it there. That was the first time Eddie and I had words.

"Where you been?" was the first thing he said to me, which I thought was downright cruel after coming all the way up that mountain the way I had. I was tired and not feeling too happy about having made that trek.

"What'd do you mean, where've I been? I just come all the way here and that's the first thing you say to me?" I was more than a little put out by the way he stood there bristling at me.

"You're three weeks late."

"Well, I been busy."

"If you knew you were going to be busy, why didn't you bring extra supplies the last time you came?"

"I . . . I just didn't think of it," I said, getting real irritated with the way he was talking to me. Seemed like he was being awfully ungrateful.

"Here," I said, putting the bags down on the porch, already starting to turn away, not liking the way he was being and thinking I'd just walk right back down the mountain again without even taking a rest. Too angry to even be thinking straight.

"Sit down for a while," Eddie said, "you're tired," and I could tell that wasn't what he really wanted to say, but he was being polite about things.

I didn't even answer him. I just trudged back and climbed up the steps and entered the cabin. I set right down in my chair.

"Get me a glass of water, would you. I'm near dying of thirst," I told him, but he didn't pay any attention to me.

He was already digging into the bag and pulling out a package of cookies. He stuffed four of them right into his mouth and started chewing. It made me sick watching him eat that way. Like he didn't have any manners at all.

"How can you eat that way, slobbering all over yourself like some kind of animal?"

Eddie didn't say anything, just glanced at me, then looked away and kept right on chewing. Soon as he was done with that first mouthful, he stuffed four more in there.

Seeing that he wasn't going to get me my water, I got out of my chair and went over to get it myself. I used the hand pump and got me a glass. Standing there drinking it, I admired the way he kept everything so clean. "You done a nice job here, son. Everything looks real good, real clean," I said, turning to look at him, thinking maybe I could smooth things out between us.

Eddie was still chewing. He took a big swallow and glared at me. "Easy to do when you don't have anything to make things dirty."

"Now what's that supposed to mean?" I glared right back.

"Forget it," he said, shaking his head and dipping his hand into the bag again.

"What'd you mean, forget it? Why don't you stop that when I'm trying to talk to you?" I asked, stepping over and slapping his hand away.

He growled at me. My boy growled at me. He'd never done that before. I took a step back and stared at him, seeing him bare those teeth. There was no smile behind them.

"I haven't eaten in four days," he said, "and before that I was living on potatoes and grub you probably wouldn't want to imagine. Don't talk to me about manners right now. Maybe later, maybe after I get something in my stomach we can talk about the finer points of etiquette," he said, still with his teeth bared.

I couldn't meet his eyes. It was almost like he knew where I'd been, as if he knew the reason I hadn't come up there hadn't had anything to with the miserable weather.

We were civil after a while. It was manageable. Later, after we'd said good-bye, I started back down the mountain. A mile or so from the cabin I passed a dog that had been ripped up and half eaten by wolves. I reminded myself that I should mention that to Eddie, make sure he knew they were around and dangerous.

Things just got progressively worse from there on. A lot of it was my fault. I didn't think, I was too busy having a good

time. I'd never been on my own and it went right to my head. I
liked going out at night and not having to be home at a certain
time or explain to anyone where I was. If I wanted to spend the
night with someone, I just went right ahead and did that, and
there were lots of nights that I didn't make it home. For the first
time since he had been born, I clean forgot about Eddie up
there on the mountainside. 'Course he was still writing his
books and they were still sending him his money. Money that I
kept for him and used just like it was my own. He'd said I could
and I did, spending it on all the things I'd ever wanted: a color
TV, a VCR, a big oak stereo cabinet with lots of CD discs I'd
put on and dance to late at night. It was the first time in my life
that everything was just working out perfectly.

How could I've acted that way? Seemed like I plain forgot
that I had a son who still needed me. I guess when I thought
about it, I was tired of being needed and wanted to do some
needing myself. It never occurred to me how much I needed
him as well. It took me a long time to remember that. Of
course, by then it seemed like I was the only one left of the two
of us who felt that way. Eddie just didn't seem to have any
family feeling left. I'd just about killed off all of that in him. It
shames me, makes me feel only more tired and depressed. I
wish I could talk to Eddie about these things, but he won't let
me near him anymore. I'd like to tell him about Mr. Dykes,
how different it is with him, how it's like it's supposed to be
with a man, not all craziness and running around like a couple
of teenagers, but I don't know if he'd listen. I don't really know
if he'll ever listen to me again.

Seems to me that, in a way, I've finally learned how to live
alone, something that Eddie's always known. And this thing
I've finally learned how to do, this thing that's taken me so long
to figure out, may have cost me my son. Though I feel so easy

about my life and how it's supposed to be, I know it wasn't worth the cost of my son. He's given me more than I've ever given him, and I've paid him back by ignoring him and trying to forget who he was. It's hard being reminded of what a foolish old woman I've become.

CHAPTER
3

I WAKE THINKING about John's letter, trying to figure out what to do about it. I light a cigarette, then glance over at the cook stove across the room, thinking how nice it would be to have a cup of coffee, but in order for that to happen I've got to get out of bed, start up the stove, then grind the beans, and wait for the water to boil. Seems like a lot of work for a cup of coffee. Be so much easier if there was someone around to just make the damn thing and bring it to me. Thinking this, I start thinking again about Alovar and women.

If I gave him a woman, he wouldn't have to do all this stuff for himself. He could get her to do it. I don't have a great deal of experience in this, but it seems to me that this is what women do.

I lie back following this thought, thinking of all the things I could get Alovar's woman to do for him. Logically I end up in the one facet of his life that has been forever absent from mine. Sex. Alovar could do all sorts of things with her, I think, imagining it, thinking of the way he could carry her off to the oasis and undress her. The way her flesh would look beneath the murky light of the wastelands sun. I wonder what kind of breasts she should have? Large, small, or just moderately sized. And what about her nipples, I wonder, and thinking this, think what the hell does it matter, as long as she has two of them and they're where they're supposed to be, everything would be just fine.

I tantalize myself with thoughts of breasts until I start to move on to other more personal parts of her anatomy. In no time at all I'm between her thighs, snuffing the sweaty scent of her, licking at the burnished copper of her private hair, and then her body opens to me and I enter her, deftly lifting and twisting her around until the smooth mounds of her buttocks press against my hips. I gently ease myself into her, feeling her hips strain against me, trying to draw me in deeper, and I explode. Alovar throws back his head in a paroxysm of pleasure.

I feel the flood of liquid splatter across my hand and stomach. I push myself out of bed, grab a paper towel, wipe myself, then trudge out the door of the cabin and around to the back. I have a hose hooked up to the pump and I shower, shivering in the morning chill.

Back inside the cabin I start the stove and begin the coffee, a process that as always seems to take forever. Finally, twenty minutes later, I've got a cup of coffee and a cigarette going and I'm standing on the porch, watching the light shaft through the tops of the trees.

I smoke, thinking about Alovar and women, wondering how the hell I'm going to be able to write about them.

Back in the cabin, I make breakfast. Six eggs, three pieces of toast, and the rest of the coffee will see me through the morning.

After breakfast, I enter the woods behind the cabin and

begin the search for wood. I'm still about two cords short of getting through the winter and the thought of it depresses me. The one thing I've come to hate more than anything else is the constant battle of wood gathering. It's the one thing I miss about civilization. There it's merely a matter of picking up the telephone book. Out here, out in my own wasteland, everything I need I pretty much have to find on my own. The old woman brings food, but trying to talk her into hauling wood up the side of the mountain probably wouldn't go over too well. Especially since I've decided not to talk to her anymore. I still blame her for the dog. I never wanted to do that, and it scared me how easily I could do it.

I take down a large hickory tree and begin cutting it down to splitting size. For a while it's pleasant, feeling the muscles in my arms and shoulders swing the ax, hearing the clean bite of it digging into the wood, but this passes quickly and leaves me sweating and growling beneath my breath.

I work at it until late morning, then begin to load up the wheelbarrow and drag it back to the house. I make four more trips before I quit for the morning. By now the sun has hit its zenith, and I grab a beer and some note paper and carry them out to the porch.

Lying down across the porch floor with my head hanging over the first step, I begin to make some notes for the new Alovar book. It won't be that much different from the previous ones, but the thought of a female character complicates things. I still can't decide if I want to do that or not. I know that it would probably boost sales, but . . .

Alovar has always disdained women. He helps them but nothing more. He has no desire for them. He's always felt that, in some obscure way, they would compromise his code. Of course there's always the other side to it. What do I know about women. Absolutely nothing. I don't know if I could write about one. My only experience with them is in what I've read, and I don't know if that would be enough. At the same time, everything I write is imagination. Couldn't I simply imagine what it would be like? This line of thought leads me back to breasts again.

I work my notes over until mid-afternoon, take a break for lunch, then go over my notes again. Satisfied with what I've done so far, I put them on my desk, to be typed that evening, then head out the cabin door.

I stretch, light a cigarette. Surveying the forests around me, I wonder which direction I should take this afternoon. Each afternoon, I try to go in a different direction. Over the years I've gotten to know the land so well that any trace of change is immediately apparent to me. At first I did this out of paranoia, afraid someone would come by and see me. But now I do it because I've come to enjoy the feel of the forest swallowing me up. It seems to take me in and turn me into something that no longer is so awkward and out of place. It gives me a sense of belonging. Maybe it's all Jack London bullshit, but I don't care. That sense of being a part of something is important to me. I'd never really had it before I came here, and now I can't imagine my life without it.

I circle the cabin and head off towards the southeast, following the trail of the sun. Soon the trees close around me, covering me in shadows. I move swiftly along the forest floor, occasionally stopping to cock my head, listening to the silence, trying to pick up any trace of sound.

I begin to run, letting my jaws slack open, chewing the air in front of me. I run for miles and stop only when I approach the base of Flag Mountain. The land veers sharply upwards into a sheer rock face that climbs for another hundred feet.

There it flattens into a small ledge, then juts upwards again for another three hundred feet to the top. The whole base of the mountain is this way. I stand at the foot of it, awkwardly twisting my head until I can see the top. I've climbed it a few times, and as far as I know am the only one since the Indians who ever has. At the top of it, I've found old Indian pottery and arrow heads. Handling the shards, thinking of the centuries they had been there until I came along to find them, to touch them, instilled in me such a sense of reverence that I found myself lifting my head and howling at the sun. The sound seemed to echo forever before it battered itself into silence in the trees.

I hunch down and light a cigarette, feeling my toes scrape at the shelf of rock only an inch beneath the earth. I smoke, listening to the sounds of birds. I'm far enough away from my cabin that they don't fear me here. I listen to their cries and long to join in with them, but know that my voice would only scare them even farther away.

Heading back I circle towards the north, checking the land, noticing the track of a squirrel, catching the scent of a rabbit, pausing at a broken branch until I discover the kind of animal that has caused it.

Four miles north of the cabin is a stream. I stop there, pull off my overalls, and wade into it, splashing myself, washing the perspiration from my body. The cold water refreshes me.

I climb out, light a cigarette, and lie on the bank watching the water rush by. Occasionally I'll spot a trout lazily drifting down the stream, exploring the moss-colored rocks, or snapping to the surface to swallow a dragonfly.

I do this until I begin to notice my reflection in the water.

It stares back at me with teeth bared. I splash it away but it returns. I rise, pull on my clothes, and begin the walk back towards my cabin, pausing now and then at a tree I've never noticed before, or a flower that seems to have sprung up overnight.

Back at the cabin the clean smell of freshly cut wood spices the air. I hunch down against the wall and light another cigarette, letting my thoughts roam the land I've just seen, thinking how much it has become a part of me. That other part of my life, that earlier part spent hidden in a small dark room, seems so far away that sometimes it seems to have happened to someone else, someone doomed to forever live in the shadows until he became a part of them. Sometimes I even find myself thinking that he's still there, that he's some distant relative that I met when I was younger and never heard from again. He's the one who put me there. Edward Talbot, Ted Talbot, my father.

My first real memory of him is of his hands. He had short stubby fingers, grained with axle grease and made strong by his work at the plant. His hands tortured me. For a long time it was all I knew of him. Hands coming into my vision, clamping around my neck, choking the air out of my lungs, until even the cry was locked in my throat. I would escape into the darkness and return to find her bending over me, cooing at me, asking me what was wrong. I still didn't have the words, and by the time I had discovered them, the hands no longer came. They had been transformed into a person. Into *him*. He would come up to see me. He would never say anything. He would only lean against the wall of the attic and look at me. The ubiquitous cigarette bobbing from the left corner of his mouth, he would stand for what seemed like hours, staring silently at me. The three points of light from his eyes and the bobbing cigarette triangulated his face, until it was a vision I saw every night in my dreams.

He never spoke to me but always seemed to be speaking about me. Late at night I would lie there listening to them below. I would hear his voice asking her what was to be done with me, and she would attempt to placate him, but he would ignore her, worrying about what would happen when they discovered me, what they would do to him, how they would persecute him.

I would listen to them and feel along the walls of the attic. Eventually I escaped into sleep. But even there he wouldn't leave me.

Far off I hear a loon cry and prick my ears forward, trying to pick up the sound again. It cries again, and then for a moment I seem to be almost able to hear its awkward wings beating the air as it pushes itself into the night sky. Unable to stop myself, I rear back and howl, letting my voice join its plaintive call.

I watch the sun disappear, then step into the cabin and begin to prepare a meal. I eat it standing by my desk. My teeth rip into the chicken, shredding bone and sucking out the marrow. For dessert I have three Oreo cookies, a cup of coffee, and a cigarette. I finish the cigarette off on the porch, watching the stars appear. I identify the ones I know and drag out the encyclopedia for the ones I don't.

Looking at the Little Dipper, I'm amazed at its delicacy. For a moment my hand rises as if to paw at it, and my gaze is drawn to the stubby, almost fur-covered hand. It seems obscene against the infinite grace of the night's constellation. I shove the hand behind my back and stargaze until the thought of Alovar draws me back into the cabin.

.   .   .

When I finally fall asleep, I dream that I am wholly human. I have a life. I even have a job I go to every day. People know me and call me by my name. They touch me, slap me on the back, ask me about football games and baseball, and I talk to them, smiling without using my teeth. I live in a house with a driveway on a tree-lined street. I even have a car and a TV set. The world is a good place. And in this dream, as I sit before my TV, a color set, I hear a knock on the door. I know it's a woman coming to visit me, a woman whom I care about and who cares about me. I rise and walk over to the door and, just as I open it, I wake.

For a moment I snuff the darkness, not sure where I am. There's a sad sense of loss when I realize there's no TV set, no home, and most definitely no woman coming to visit. There's only my own stale breath and the chill of the cabin. I grunt, reach out, and light up. The smoke offers me a little companionship but not quite enough to clear away the depression.

I curl up, thinking what it would be like to have the life I dreamed. I give it up when I realize I can't even imagine it. Me, the great science fiction writer—or at least adequate one— can't even muster enough imagination to picture such a life.

I find myself thinking about John and wondering what he would think if he ever knew who was sending him those manuscripts. We've never met. Everything we do is by mail. The one time he wrote, telling me to call him, I wrote back explaining that I had a profound distrust of telephones. Better that he think I'm eccentric.

Sleep drifts away from me. I rise, wrap the comforter around me, step out onto the porch, and watch the darkness slowly draw back. I start the cook stove and prepare a pot of coffee, then go back outside. I walked around to the back of the cabin and watch the sun rise. Its first light hits and warms me. I bask in it, feeling my muscles loosen, then I stretch hugely and yawn into the dawning light.

I pour a cup of coffee and hunker down on the porch, feeling tired but not tired enough to try going back to sleep. I think about Alovar and what I should have him do today. My mind pauses, then moves on to thoughts of a woman. I'm still not sure what to do about that, but it's something I can leave alone for a while.

First I'll let him kill some people before I think some more about it. I've discovered that people love to read that kind of stuff, which is what my books are filled with. Great battles and glorious quests. It seems to be a need that everyone has. And thinking this, I examine myself, trying to find some battle or quest that interests me. The only possible quest I can come up with is a TV set. It's the one thing I would love to have, my one desire, but without electricity it seems impossible. I've thought about putting a generator in but the sheer logistics of getting one up here seem unmanageable. The old woman could never do it. And, since I'm not speaking to her, it makes the whole thing even more difficult to figure out.

It would be nice, I think, to have other faces up here. Lots of clean, pure faces, talking to one another. The sound of other voices would also be pleasant, something other than the plangent whine of the old woman begging forgiveness. Sometimes, when she's not around, I can almost bring myself to forgive her. But once she gets here, once she's actually at my door, I find the sound and smell of her so annoying that it's all I can do not to rush out growling at her.

I light a cigarette, rubbing my flank against the cabin wall, letting the wood dig into the muscle and bone. I think of the old woman and her treachery, and then I think of the dog and am ashamed. I can't seem to separate one from the other.

If she had only come up that time, if she had even told me she would be late, maybe I could have stopped myself. But the not knowing, the sudden realization that maybe she would never come again, drove me insane. It turned me into what I look like. And having never before realized what I was capable of becoming, it terrified me beyond anything I had ever known. Even her husband never instilled in me such horror as what I felt crouched down over the body of the dog, rending huge strips of flesh from its body, gobbling them down in a gluttonous feast. And after realizing what I had done, what I could become, I vomited it all up. Spitting up the bitter bile of fur and uncooked flesh, spewing it across my own matted chest.

I shake the thoughts away, shivering in the cold, thinking of the old woman and her men. The scent of them on her body. The scent of so many of them on her body.

Now it's different, but not different enough for me to forgive her. How can I ever forgive her for what she showed me about myself? Especially since she is responsible for what I am. It was her choice and she accepted it. Sooner she had murdered me at first sight, than her pretense that I don't exist. I do exist, but my existence is so tentatively defined that without her I am doomed to become what I seem.

I rise and refill my coffee cup. I think of gathering wood, then glance over at the bed and the new books the old woman brought. I walk to the bed and lie down on my side, taking a book with me. I keep my cup within reach and open the book.

I let the words take me and soon I am a part of them. I live in a normal town among normal people who talk about sports and politics and get upset. No one knows about the woods and the wasteland, none of them suspects what lives on the fringe of the mountains. They fill their lives with petty worries about mortgages and the dent in their new car. I let myself become a part of them until I live next door and watch everything they do from my window. In front of me, in color, is a huge TV set. I watch and listen, thinking how good life can be. I let the day pass by without me.

Evening finds me dull and sluggish. Lack of physical activity has only increased my lethargy. Rather than fight it, I wallow in it. Whimpering at the cold, groaning at the drudgery of having to make up a meal, I stand at my desk, fingering pages and pages of notes about Alovar, and stuff cold chicken in my mouth. I wash it down with a can of beef barley soup.

I glance at the typewriter, then growl at it, thinking about the effort it requires. An expenditure of energy that I don't feel capable of this evening. I push Alovar away and stride to the sink, carrying my dirty dish. I wash it quickly and set it to dry, then turn and look around my cabin. The four walls seem warm and secure. The idea of going outside is not particularly inviting.

I take a cigarette and step over to my battery-operated radio. I flip on a station out of California that plays light rock. The music seems much too effete for my mood. I flip around until I find something with a little blood and guts to it. It's a group called, obscenely enough, The Revolting Cocks, and the chorus screams out, "Beer, steers, and queers. Ye haw!" The sound of it invigorates me. I find myself joining in each time the chorus comes around, screaming it out discordantly with the group. I turn the volume up until the music blasts the walls of the cabin and bounces back from the rafters. Soon it has me dancing wildly around the room. I leap in the air, windmilling my arms from side to side, finally feeling my blood begin to flow.

I thrash around the cabin, moving with a grace no normal human has ever known. Shifting parts of my body that aren't even possessed by those outside my boundaries. I glory in the music, finding a certain element of revolt in its primal beat. When the song concludes, I pause, gasping for breath in a corner of the room, waiting for the next cut. Foetus is the name of the group, and they kick in with a such a cacophonous drum roll that I'm off again before I even know what I'm doing.

I dance for hours, throwing myself from one end of the cabin to the other, howling. My blood boils in my veins. My teeth bared, arms lifted backwards to the ceiling, legs and claws scraping the floorboards, I know I'm a picture of grace no ballet dancer could ever emulate.

At last, out of breath, covered in sweat, I flip off the radio and lean panting against my desk. As my frenzy ebbs, I hear the sound of my own lungs, rasping, animal-like. It sounds loud in the silence of the cabin. The sound offends. It reminds me too much of what I am. I grab a cigarette and rush outside, into the night, where my sound is cushioned by the pine and ponderosa trees.

I inhale hugely, taking in the scents, then light my cigarette, drawing it deep into my lungs, finding a certain pleasure in the twinge of pain it gives. Pain, I've found, sometimes releases me back into reality. I've often thought that I know exactly why Van Gogh cut off his ear. He did it to feel something, anything. He had become so abstracted from reality that the mere act of mutilation, and the attendant pain, would ground him again, he hoped, would shock him into feeling what being human was like.

I've never had to go that far, probably because I can't go that far. Humanity is something that will always be denied me, no matter what I feel or what I think. A man is defined by the composite of his physical form.

In Salem, during the witch trials, a woman with a third nipple was considered to have entered into a pact with the devil. If discovered, she would burn at the stake. In Turkey, in the last century, a person with a cataract was reputed to carry the evil eye and was shunned. In the late 1800s a baby born in Wyoming with six fingers on one hand was immediately suffocated and burned. In the southern United States, any black was considered both threatening and inferior. He was liable to be found guilty of any possible crime, regardless of culpability.

A man is not what he is but what he is perceived to be. Visible form is the definition of a man's humanity. Give me a world of the blind and maybe I would have a chance. Take my eyes and let me join them. Let me, just for one day, one hour, be a part of them, and I'll gladly go back to the woods, to my cabin, to this wasteland that I've come to inhabit so well. If I could only . . .

I pause, forcing myself to stop. These are things I've contemplated countless times before. They serve no purpose, other than to frustrate and enrage me. It's pointless. You are what you eat. You are what you are and as others see you. It can't be any other way. I am what I appear to be. I am a monster.

The woods glisten beneath the stars. I stare off, inhaling the fecund scent of the earth, and put my cigarette out beneath the pad of my foot. I lope gracefully across my front yard into the trees, glorying in this reversion to what I really am, and the irrefutable proof of my own bestiality. Let the puny normals decry everything about me, but they can never take this from me.

I move easily through the underbrush, my nostrils bringing me scents from far off. Squirrel, rabbit, a pheasant, and, a little to the northeast, a deer. I pause, head thrown back, taking in this scent, imagining the movements of the animal as it bows its head and rips tufts of grass from the base of a tree.

I move farther into the woods and stop at the edge of a clearing. The ground is matted and beaten hard. I've stood here before. Far off I can see the dim lights of a town. The town where the old woman lives.

Standing here, I throw my head back and exhale hugely, then inhale through my nostrils, taking in vast amounts of air, isolating in each eddy the scents. The distant aroma of wood smoke and oil, the subtle odor of people—sweat, the acrid stench of blood, and more fragile, barely discernible, the scent of perfume. A distant flowery scent that subtly infiltrates my senses, and leaves me with the knowledge that, if I linger too long, it will surely drive me mad.

I turn back into the woods and run, occasionally dropping to all fours, throwing my head back to howl at the night eyes staring down at me, challenging them in some atavistic manner that even I don't understand.

I crawl back into my cabin and burrow beneath my blankets, shaking from the cold and the memory of the perfumed smells that rose from the town far below.

When I sleep, I dream, and what I dream is the house, the house that I occupy only in my sleep: the TV, the people who call and visit, the job, and the knocking at the door that announces my visitor. As always, I rise to answer the door and the dream ends, twirling me back into the woods, where I crouch over the carcass of the dog.

I scream and can't tell if the scream is a part of the dream or part of me. For a moment I wake, still hearing the scream. Before I can decide if it's real or not, I fall back asleep and dream nothing.

CHAPTER
4

FOR FOUR DAYS Alovar traveled across the burnt lands, seeing nothing but the crusted earth around him. There was no foliage, no sound of bird or animal, only Alovar, driven by an impulse he could not identify.

The land was vast and empty. Nothing upset its flat horizon. On the morning of the fourth day, far off to the west, Alovar could just make out the dim shadow of a structure. Energized by this sighting, he walked more quickly.

He walked without letting up, his eyes locked on this growing vision in the distance. By noontime he could make out other structures, scattered around the larger one. The shimmering heat, rising from the sand, made it difficult for him to truly identify this vision. He pushed on, anxious to see what it might be.

For years Alovar had heard the tales of the burnt lands. How there was nothing out there, and the few who managed to return from this journey came back with the wasting death in their veins. Alovar had believed none of this. He had learned at a very early age that only what he could see with his own eyes was worthy of belief.

By late afternoon he could make out the taller structure. It was the shell of an old building. He pushed on, disregarding his thirst and his hunger, promising himself he would appease both once he reached this oasis.

Late evening found Alovar at the foot of the structure, staring up at it in awe. Its sheer size was beyond anything he had ever seen: it rose hundreds of feet in the air. And even in its present disrepair, it still managed a grace that directed the eyes' movement as he had never before experienced.

Exhausted, Alovar quickly surveyed his surroundings. Satisfied that all seemed secure, Alovar spread his ground sheet and, without eating or drinking, fell into a heavy sleep.

His dreams were a turmoil of images and structures he could not understand. Majestic buildings, vast amounts of people, and over-riding them all was the sound of thousands and thousands of voices. It was a dream world found only in sleep. It no longer existed, couldn't have existed. It was too large, too filled with life, to imagine such a reality in the present world.

His was one filled with disease and small pockets of humanity in disarray, struggling against their own mortality and the Marauders that preyed on every living thing. Even in the Realm there was no certain safety. Alovar himself, by the age of sixteen, had fought eight times in the Box. Each time victorious, until soon, at only eighteen, he was elevated to the Circle Guard and from there to the Circle itself. For eight years he had remained a part of the Circle and probably would have remained for eight more if not for Staron. It was Staron who first began the rumor, commenting on Alovar's comely looks and how it seemed that Alovar never appeared to age. Soon all who encountered him began to examine him closely, always doing this obliquely, knowing the strength of Alovar's sword and the speed of its delivery.

"A man who doesn't age. A man who shows no signs of the Circle's hardships," Staron would reason, to any who would listen. "How can this be a man? He must certainly be one of the mutants,"

Staron would conclude, looking knowingly at his audience. "One of the uncivilized."

Alovar knew of these rumors but paid them no heed, thinking, unwisely, that this would soon pass and that Staron's words would be seen for the canard they were.

But this is not what happened.

Staron's words grew stronger with each retelling, until soon there was little doubt in anyone's mind about their veracity. By the time Alovar deigned to answer these charges, there was no one who would listen.

Attacked and bound while he slept, Alovar was dragged before the high court of the Circle.

"He is not a man!" screamed Staron. "He is a barbarian, sent among us to seek our weaknesses. He will destroy us all and throw us into savagery!" Staron pointed with a flourish to Alovar, who stood bracketed by guards. "Look at him. How is it possible that anyone can look like him? Look at his features, look closely," Staron said, touching him lightly on the cheek, the forehead, and the top of his head. "No man touched by the rays can look like this."

Alovar stared out at the court, meeting their eyes, set in scarred, wrinkled flesh. He thought of his own body, strong, unblemished by age or combat, and for a moment found a certain truth in Staron's words.

"I will show you," Staron said. "I reveal a truth before all who watch me." He turned back to Alovar, and for a moment Alovar glimpsed something in the other's gaze he could not identify.

Staron drew his sword and placed its tip against Alovar's cheek, then said, "Behold," and drew the tip of the sword down Alovar's face.

Alovar felt the sword tip bend against his flesh, and knew that it was no ordinary weapon but one of the jester's, used for play.

He opened his mouth to speak, but Staron quickly whispered, "Exile or death, pretty one. I offer exile. Open your mouth and it shall be death." Then he turned quickly back to the court.

"No wound, no blood. This is not a man. This is a mutant. One of the barbarians who has been sent among us to pollute and destroy us," Staron screamed, waving his arm feverishly at Alovar.

The judges stared in astonishment at Alovar's unmarked cheek.

"I say exile him. Throw him back to his own people. Let him be the savage he is."

Alovar met the eyes of the court and saw the hardening expression of each of them, and knew what his fate would be.

"Why not death?" one of the judges asked.

"It is too easy," Staron shrugged. "With his beauty, he will become a plaything for the barbarians' desires."

Alovar was dragged from the court to a cell. For three days he was left there, unfed, unwashed, and ignored. On the fourth day, Staron appeared.

"You are to be exiled. You will be taken to the edge of the Realm and released to the land."

"Why?" rasped Alovar, clinging to the bars, meeting the other's gaze.

Staron's eyes were the first to drop away. "You are too perfect. Perfection," Staron said, shaking his head sadly, "is not possible any longer. It is better not to see what we can't be, when it is all important that we strive for what we can be." He paused, then turning back to meet Alovar's eyes, reached up and gripped his hand. "We do this for the Circle. We do this in the hope that one day we might be like you."

He mounted the stairs. At the top, without turning, Staron spoke his last words to Alovar. "Tomorrow at sunrise you shall be released to the land. Return only if you seek death."

Huddled in a corner of his cell, Alovar tried to understand

Staron's meaning. To be exiled, even to die for the Circle, was a judgment Alovar could accept. But to die needlessly, without benefit to anyone, Alovar could not accept.

He knew his appearance was extraordinary. The thick shock of blond hair falling over his unlined forehead had more than once cause consternation among his peers. His piercing blue eyes and jutting cheek bones had earned the smiles of more than one Circle maiden, but these things were accidents of birth. Alovar could trace his line back three generations and never once had there been a hint of tainted blood. His birth was no more than a fortuitous timing of sun and moon. To be condemned for these things, to be pushed from civilized society for the betterment of the Circle, made no sense to him. In what way would his banishment help the Realm? And conversely, how could his remaining in the Realm do damage to it? If what Staron said was true, if his appearance distracted and negated the desire for perfection, then what would happen to people when they attained perfection? Would they be doomed to destroy it once it was accomplished? Is that what had happened to the old world? Was perfection too potent for humans to view? And if it was, if all that Staron said was true, then what place was there for Alovar in this world?

At sunrise the next morning he was stripped of clothes and weapons, taken to the boundaries of the Realm, and released. Followed by the eyes of his peers and friends, Alovar turned and made his way into this new world.

Only after he was far from their view did he fall to his knees, cursing the gods that had condemned him to inhabit such a body as his. The Marauders found him this way, bent over on the sand, raking his face and chest with his nails. Despite his disheveled appearance, they were amazed by the sight of this comely youth, and set upon him hungrily.

Naked, armed only with rage, Alovar exploded. It was over in moments. Two of the Marauders lay sprawled across the arid ground, their necks twisted into unnatural positions. A third, cradling his right arm, attempted to crawl away.

Alovar clothed and armed himself and, with one backward glance, disappeared into his new world.

For eight years Alovar traveled this territory. During that time his reputation grew from rumor to legend. Even in the Circle there was talk of this warrior who roamed the land, meting out swift punishment to those who abused the helpless, and offering assistance to those who were in need.

Alovar, still without the faintest hint of aging, had begun to question the nature of the World. His views, once aligned with the Realm, were now nearly opposed to that kingdom. He no longer saw it as the last bastion of civilization, but began to wonder if it wasn't the last stronghold of barbarity. What could be more barbaric than to leave a full three-quarters of your population to wander a land without hope, without any goal in mind? Preyed upon by the Marauders, abused for their physical deformities, Alovar found these people—the mutants—more akin to himself than any he had met in the Realm. His own deformity, his beauty, seemed as grotesque as theirs.

A L O V A R awoke at the foot of the edifice. After a breakfast of hard bread and dried meat, he rose and set off to examine the other structures around him. They were like nothing he had ever seen. The shells of old buildings were never in such shape as these. Many seemed completely untouched by time or vandals. And as he walked among them, Alovar felt as though he were the first living thing to have done so in a long time.

Off to the side of the largest structure, which he had seen from the desert, he found a smaller building made of a curious blend of stone and sand. The door, a wooden one, hung broken from a metal hinge. Drawing his sword, Alovar entered.

The floor of the main room consisted of the same material as the walls. It was cracked in places and covered with a fine layer of dust. Alovar walked cautiously to the center of the room and surveyed the strange interior. On the wall facing him was a large painting of a huge body of water, and on this water were boats, enormous white boats with billowing sheets that hung from a large beam running vertically from the center. Alovar stepped to the wall and examined the scene almost reverently. The water seemed to go on endlessly, marred only by the graceful ships.

The River Dirge, which ran through the center of the Realm, was barely the width of the awkward boats that navigated its shallow bed. But this, Alovar thought, looking at the scene before him, this was beyond anything imaginable.

He ran his hand over the face of the painting, feeling the grit of ages beneath his fingers, and tried to imagine a world that could hold such wonders. It was beyond his comprehension.

He stepped away and examined the rest of the room.

Various objects for sitting were strewn along one wall. Some were of such strange design that only after examining them at length could he begin to understand their function. He sat in one and was amazed that anything built so crooked, so bent, could be so comfortable. He lounged back, his sword resting on his knee, and looked around this stone room, trying to picture what manner of men once ruled there. Would they have looked like him, or would they have resembled the mutants, disfigured and deformed. And what of their languages and their governments? Were they ruled wisely? he wondered. Then rising and stepping outside to look at the wasteland surrounding him, he realized that no, they could not have been ruled too wisely since they had come to this.

Alovar spent the morning and afternoon exploring the city. He saw buildings that appeared completely untouched by whatever catastrophe had overtaken this ancient civilization. Inside them he found things for which he had no words. He would pick them up, examine them closely, then gently return them to their place, thinking that some day he would learn the use of these objects.

In one building he found a paper book, buried beneath a curious gray ash. Gingerly, he picked it up and examined it. Looking at the face of it, he knew that these scribbles must be their language. He had seen language written in the Realm. The Sanctuarians wrote in the Realm Chambers, chronicling the history of the Realm. It was their life's work; they gave their souls as well as their manhood for the privilege of their position. He had seen these weighty books in the Circle's chambers, but only the Sanctuarians could decipher the figures inside. It was their right by royal decree, and it was a right they guarded jealously. Alovar had never heard of anyone, other than a Sanctuarian, who knew the mystery of these figures.

For a moment, holding the book in his hand, he felt an urge to put it down, knowing that even to look at the interior of this book was a transgression. He shook this thought off, remembering the day he had been loosed, cast out naked and unarmed, past the last boundary of civilized society.

He turned a page and was amazed. A picture. He gasped and stepped back, his sword rising automatically. A woman. Tall and blond, a woman whose face was filled with beauty. She was clothed in a black dress that fell to her ankles. Her feet, small and shapely, peeked out from beneath the edge of the dress like two pink animals.

Alovar stared at her, seeing the way the dress tightened around her bust and hips. He glanced at her hands, looking for the deformity he knew must be there. One held a bottle and one a goblet, and each was perfectly formed. The long slender fingers had a startling dash of red at the end of each.

Alovar backed up against a chair and sat, paging through the book eagerly, seeing things he never thought possible. Vehicles without horses. Machines that seemed to hang in the air, and everywhere throughout the pages—people. People like he had never imagined. Beautiful people with startling white teeth and full heads of hair, all of them smiling. For hours he examined this book, finding a sense of magic in it. It was only as he felt the shadows outside that he managed to pull himself to his feet and leave the building.

The sun glimmered opaquely on the western horizon, giving everything an orange hue. Alovar carefully clamped the book beneath his arm and walked back to his camp. There he made a small fire, brewed his tea, and ate. He pored over the paper pages again, entranced by this vision of another place.

Hours later, when he curled up beside the dying embers of his fire, he slept and dreamt of it. And as he entered these dreams, he knew in his heart, though not in his mind, that these people, these beautiful people from so long ago, had given him the gift of their beauty.

HE WOULDN'T COME out again, no matter how much I begged. I left the stuff for him just like I always do, and then I walked away and hid up in the rocks, watching. He came out moments later and stared off in the direction I had gone. He huffed once, then bent over and picked up the packages and carried them into the cabin. I knew what that huff meant, and I wished there was some way I could have called out to him, but I know how he gets when he's like this. That boy can hold a grudge just about forever. No use my trying to talk to him until he's ready to talk. Going up the mountain I always tell myself that, but it seems like once I actually get there, and I'm standing right in front of his door, I just can't seem to help myself. I know it's not going to do one bit of good, but I keep right on asking him to come out, just for a while. Seems like all the Talbots are a little bit addled, one way or another.

This is my son: those were the words that I kept thinking over and over again all the way down that mountain. Sometimes I'd think them and they'd be angry words, and other times I'd think them and they would seem like they were the saddest words ever.

Marilyn called a while ago to ask me about my leg, which was nice of her. It's nice to have someone who thinks about you when you're not around. I wonder if Eddie ever does while he's writing on his books and whatever else. Does he ever stop and think about how things used to be? Not towards the end, when Ted went crazy, but the times we used to spend together up in the attic, me holding him on my lap, with a book in one hand and the other wrapped around his furry little waist, does he remember that? Or does he just remember all those other ugly goings-on?

There's nothing I can do about them. Those happened and I'll be the first to admit that I was stupid, but it doesn't do any good knowing that if the person I hurt won't even listen to me. I wonder if Eddie even knows what it is to hurt someone? I've never seen him do anything like that. I've never seen him hurt anything—insect, animal, or even human. Eddie's about the gentlest person I ever knew, and that's not because he's my son but because it's true. Sometimes when I think of him being that way, it makes me wonder about the whole world and how crazy it all is. Everybody always walking around hurting everybody else and just living a fine old life, while Eddie's hidden up there on the side of the mountain and he never hurt no one or nothing, yet he can't even live any kind of normal life. Doesn't seem fair, but as Ted used to say, you can't expect fair. Ain't nothing fair that don't sell cotton candy.

Mr. Dykes came over last night to see how I was doing. We had a real nice time. He brought over a video of *It's a Wonderful Life,* and I made some popcorn and we sat down and watched the movie together.

That one part still makes me cry. Seems stupid that it can still do that to me after all the times I've seen it, but it just plugs right into my eyes and I can't stop myself. Maybe it's because of that one time I watched it with Eddie.

Eddie was all excited over getting to see TV. Seemed like there were mighty few occasions that he got to do that. Only when Ted went off somewhere on a hunting trip or the like. Ted didn't think he should watch television. He said it'd just give the boy ideas, and didn't make no sense in doing that to someone who couldn't afford to have any ideas. I think Ted always expected Eddie to just disappear in the attic. I remember he'd go up there and not come back for hours. And when he did he'd just look at me and shake his head, like he couldn't believe what he'd seen. I always wanted to tell him that was his son up there, his own flesh and blood that he was mistreating, but I never did. Maybe that was stupid. It gets so it's hard to tell after a while what is and what isn't.

But that time with Eddie, setting the TV up in the corner of his attic, the two of us on his bed, Eddie curled up across my stomach—just thinking about that, I can almost feel the warmth of the boy again. But then, when I do, and I realize that he isn't there anymore, it feels so cold, I don't want to even remember it.

Anyway, it was right after Jimmy Stewart jumped off the bridge and was in the gatekeeper's hut that Eddie got all excited. Jimmy Stewart suddenly realizing he could hear out of his good ear, and the angel Clarence was saying, "Why, you've never been born, Mr. Bailey," and Eddie started cheering and jumping up and down.

I tried to explain to him that, now that Jimmy Stewart hadn't been born, he didn't have anything—all his family was gone, and all of his friends. And Eddie looked right back at me with his teeth bared and, nodding his head all excited like, said, "But he can start over, Mom. He can start all over and be something different."

Even towards the end, when Jimmy Stewart's running down the streets saying hello to everything, Eddie didn't get it. He thought Jimmy was better off before. And at the very end, when they're all standing around singing, Eddie looked at me and asked, "But what about the eight thousand dollars, Mom. Does the old man get to keep that, too." Like there was nothing that was happy about the movie, and even that little thing wasn't fair.

I guess when I see the film now and the tears start washing down my cheeks, it's as much for Jimmy Stewart as for Eddie.

I hated Eddie's favorite movie, *A Clockwork Orange.* How could you like something like that? I would ask him. And Eddie would bare his teeth and shake his shaggy head at me like I was some kind of fool, and only say he thought it was an amusing story. I never could understand that one part where the boy's singing that Gene Kelly song and kicking that old man in the head. How could anyone like that? That's when I started worrying about Eddie and what it was doing to him being locked up in the attic. Only time he ever got to see anybody was out on the highway behind the house. There was that one little triangular window in the back of his room that looked out towards the road. The older he got, the more I'd catch him standing there, staring at the cars going by. Sometimes he'd see hitchhikers and tell me all about it when I'd go upstairs to visit. He'd ask all sorts of questions. How come they were wearing this or that, and where did they all go after the cars picked them up? He'd make me go to the library and get travel books so he could try to understand.

I talked to Ted about it, told him I thought we had to do

something about the boy, it wasn't right keeping him up there all the time. And Ted, he just stared at me a long time and said, "Well, what do you think we should do, send him to school?" Then he kind of grunted and lighted one of those cigarettes of his.

I said, "We got to do something with him. Can't we let him go outside at night when no one can see him?"

"Shit, how can we let something like *him* outside? No telling what he'd do once he got free." Ted just walked away.

It wasn't until later, after I'd thought about what he'd said, that I realized what he meant. I always thought we were protecting Eddie from other people. We both knew what would happen if people saw him. They'd never understand that Eddie was just built a little differently. Didn't make no difference that, in Eddie's mind, he was just like everyone else. He was probably a whole lot smarter than most. Reason we had him up there, I thought, was so he wouldn't get hurt. But after thinking about what Ted had said, I realized Ted didn't think of it that way.

He saw Eddie as some kind of monster.

I guess I'd known that but just never admitted it to myself. And even then I couldn't quite make myself accept it. If I had, everything would have been a lot different.

Mr. Dykes started telling me about his niece, who's come to visit him. Said he was wondering if I would mind meeting her. That sounded a little odd to me, so I asked him right out, "What do you mean, would I mind meeting her? Why on earth would I?" I said, looking at him closely.

He got all sheepish and kind of looked away for a moment

before he turned back and said, "Well, Annie, she's had some troubles, and Barbara thought it might be good if she came up here to stay with me for a little while."

Although I don't really think of myself as a snoopy person, the way he said that, there was no way I was going to leave it alone.

"What kind of troubles she been having?" I asked.

"Oh, just some problems. Nothing really important. Kid things," Mr. Dykes said.

"Kids sure can get themselves into stuff," I agreed.

"Yes, that's certainly true," Mr. Dykes sighed.

We sat on the porch rocker for a few moments longer, sipping our lemonade, before I asked, "What kind of stuff are we talking about exactly?"

For a moment I didn't think he was going to answer, then he smiled, nudging me with a shoulder, and said, "You sure are a nosy one, aren't you?"

I grinned right back at him and said, "Seems to me, way you said that, you're looking for a little bit of nose in your business."

"I tell you what," he said, "let me bring her round tomorrow and you see what you think of her. I don't want you to be prejudiced by some of what she's done before, okay?"

I nodded, then asked him if I was going to have to lock up my valuables. He grinned and said, "Seems to me you don't have much of value in that old house of yours, excepting yourself of course."

He winked when he said that, but neither of us was much fooled by it. We both knew where we stood, his wanting to and my not wanting to were things we talked about before. It was hard talking to him about those things and not bringing Eddie into it, because Eddie was the whole reason we weren't more

serious than we were. If it weren't for Eddie, I think Mr. Dykes
and I would have already tied the knot. He'd asked often
enough, and I was more than sure that he was a good, caring
man, but with Eddie up there, depending on me, there was
nothing I could say but no. I couldn't leave the boy alone again.
I'd done it once out of sheer foolishness, and I sure wasn't
going to do it again, no matter what the reason.

Next day, Mr. Dykes brought her over. Katherine's her
name, though she answers only to Kat—she told me that right
off when he introduced us. I didn't have much to say, I was still
looking at her hair, trying to figure out how a person could get
it to be that color. I never seen hair like that before. Kind of an
orange and purple color, with bits of yellow in it. And the sides
were all shaved off into streaks that showed right down to her
scalp. I stared for a while, unable to take my eyes away from her
hair. Then I looked up at Mr. Dykes and he was just smiling
and nodding at me like she was the most ordinary person in the
world. She might have been, but it sure wasn't any place I knew
of.

We all stood there for a little while, me staring at that hair
of hers, Mr. Dykes smiling, and Kat peering around behind
me, trying to peek into the rest of my house, before I remembered my manners.

"Come on in, make yourself at home," I said, stepping
back, and waving them inside.

Kat moved through that door like she was being chased by
an unchained dog. Mr. Dykes came right behind her, still
smiling. I examined that smile real close, trying to figure out
exactly what kind it was. Seemed like there was a little bit more
than just friendliness in it. Maybe a little more of it was aimed
in my direction than a normal smile should have been.

By the time I turned back to the room, Kat was already

over by the sideboard, looking at all the pictures, picking them up and examining them, front and back.

"Who're all these people? Seem like they're real old," she said, turning to me.

Her hair didn't move at all when she moved. It just stood straight up on her head like a rooster's cowl. Made me want to touch it to see what it felt like.

"Mostly family."

"Wow, look at this guy, Uncle Jake," she said, carrying a picture over to Mr. Dykes.

I looked over his shoulder at a picture of my grandfather standing by the barn.

"He looks like he's about a hundred years old. How old is he, anyway?"

"Well, he must've been about seventy-four when we took that one. That's the old barn back there. It burned down in—"

I stopped when she turned away abruptly and went back to the sideboard. I glanced over and caught Mr. Dyke's eye. He shrugged but still kept that smile of his in place.

"Man, these sure are old. They must be worth something, I bet. In L.A. they'd pay a fortune for stuff like this. They like all that dead stuff. Not me, though. I like things that are more new, that still have the glitter on them."

Kat moved to the bureau by the window.

"You're from California then?"

"Yep. Didn't Jake tell you?" Kat paused to look at me for a moment, then returned to her examination of my bureau top.

"No, I don't think he did mention that, did you, Jake?" I said, putting a little weight onto the Jake.

"Must have slipped my mind," he answered, not meeting my eye.

Well, after Kat had inspected most of the living room, she

sat down on the sofa while I brought out some iced tea. Watching her sip it, I could tell she was just dying to go through the rest of the house. She kept glancing off behind me at the hallway leading to the bedrooms. I asked her about California, and it seemed like every time I did, Mr. Dykes would supply the answers for her.

I finally managed to ask her what she thought about the town.

"I hate it," she said without pausing.

"How come?"

"Well, jeez, what's to like about it? There's nothing to do here, there's not even a theater."

"It's got the mountains, and I think they're about the prettiest things I've ever seen," I said. Mr. Dykes was nodding right along with me.

"What's the big deal about mountains," Kat shrugged. "You seen one you seen 'em all. They don't do anything. They just sit there and look good. I'd rather be on Rodeo Drive. Least there, people who look good have put some time into it. Here, all this stuff just exploded out of the ground a million years ago and hasn't done anything since." Having concluded, she drained her iced tea.

I refilled her glass, trying to think of something to say to that. Not much came to mind.

"Kat's going to be with me until next spring," Mr. Dykes finally said.

"What about school?" I asked. "Are you going to go to the high school here?"

Kat laughed like I'd told her the best joke she'd ever heard. "I'm out of school. I quit last year. Mom and Dad sent me up here to punish me."

"Now, Kat, you know that's not true."

"Yeah they did, Jake, you know that. There's no sense in trying to hide it. Annie probably knows it all anyway, don't you?" she asked, looking right at me.

"Mr. Dykes hasn't said anything to me about that," I said, feeling flustered.

" 'Mr. Dykes'—you always call him 'Mr. Dykes'? How come you don't call him Jake?"

"Well, when I was younger—" I started to explain.

"Seems crazy to me, the way the two of you are and all, that you don't call him by his first name." Kat looked at the two of us, each sneaking looks at the other, me wondering what he had said to her, and he wondering how I was going to take that.

"Try it," said Kat. "Just say it once. I heard you say it before, but I think you said it then because you were mad or something. Go ahead, say it."

What else could I do. "Jake," I said, and then for the life of me, I don't know why, I giggled.

"See, that wasn't so bad. I think you should call him Jake from now on. It's crazy to call him Mr. Dykes. That's just stupid, right?"

I nodded, looking at her a little more closely now, able to see more of her than just her hair. She was kind of a homely thing, once you got past that hairdo, but she wasn't ugly. Her eyes were her best feature. They were that deep blue color that goes on forever. Her nose was a little too big and her chin seemed to jut out a little bit more than it should, but that didn't make all that much difference, because it was so hard to concentrate on her face. She seemed to be constantly fidgeting, eyes always darting around, her legs bouncing up and down, or she was fingering the gold chain that hung from her earlobe.

They stayed for a hour or so before Jake announced they had to get home to prepare supper. Kat made a face behind his back. When I asked her about this, she said that she did all the "preparing" while Jake took a nap.

"What're you making?" I asked, wondering what kind of food this girl would cook.

"Tofu and bean sprouts." Seeing my expression, she explained what it was. Didn't sound like much in the way of food, but I nodded and told her that it sounded interesting.

"It's okay. Jake hates it too, but it's good for him," she said, then put an arm around Jake's shoulders and squeezed him. It surprised me when she did that. It was the first time I realized how much she really did like him. And the way he glanced over at her, I could tell he felt the same way about her.

Watching the two of them walk down the sidewalk together, I suddenly noticed the way she always looked right at him when she talked to him. She hadn't done that with me. Her eyes seemed to flit all over the house, even when she was asking me a question. Her gaze never stayed for any longer than a second on my face. But with Jake, she listened closely and seemed to take in what he was saying. Half the time when I'd been talking to her, I wondered if she'd even heard what I'd been saying.

Jake called later to ask how I was feeling, and we talked for a while, neither of us mentioning her, though I knew that was what he wanted to hear. Reason I didn't comment on her was I didn't know what to think of her.

He never came right out and asked, so I just never brought it up. He asked if he could come by tomorrow afternoon, but I told him no, I was busy with the church and wouldn't be free until the evening. Maybe tomorrow evening he could stop by if he liked. Then he kind of asked if he could bring Kat along. That would be fine with me, I told him, if she wanted to come. It surprised me when he said that she did, that she liked me. I never would have thought it. Seemed to me that whatever that girl felt, she kept pretty well hidden.

My leg's bad. It scares me some to think about it. If it gets worse, I don't know what I'm going to do about Eddie. Who'll bring his things up to him if I can't? Sometimes it makes me wish that Ted was around, not the Ted I knew at the end but the one I knew at the beginning. The Ted that used to pick me up in his old Chevy Nova and seemed to enjoy himself so much. Seemed like everything he did then was fun, no matter what it was.

Even right at the beginning, when we were first married and money was kind of scarce, Ted always seemed to find something to be happy about. When I first started to show, Ted would lie beside me at night and put his head on my stomach, and tell me it was going to be the prettiest baby the county ever did see. After Eddie, everything changed. Ted never smiled anymore. That part of him just up and disappeared like it had never even been there.

Sometimes when I'm feeling sorry for myself and my leg's acting up, I think about what it would have been like if Eddie had been different. Would Ted have turned out differently too, or was that hardness always inside him, just waiting for something to uncover it?

My knee's all swollen up and it hurts worse than ever. It's never been this bad before. It worries me. Doc Calken told me, if it kept getting worse, they were going to have to operate. I think next week I better start bringing up extra supplies for Eddie, just in case. I wished he'd talk to me, even if it was only to yell.

CHAPTER

6

FOR THE FOURTH morning in a row I wake up thinking about the old woman. It bothers me that I do this. I'm tired of dwelling on her but, after the last visit, I know I have to.

I could smell her long before she arrived, that scent that's all her own. A blend of lilacs, soap, old woman's sweat, and something new this time, something that frightened me—a subtle whiff of pain. She carried it on her like a perfume. I picked up on it right away, and it brought me over to the window long before she appeared at the head of the path.

I stood there, waiting until she appeared on the ridge and began to limp her way down, pulling the two-wheeled wagon behind her. The closer she got, the stronger the odor. And what made it all so much worse was knowing how the pain had started.

She came up to the door, just like always, and unloaded the bags. When she was done, she sat down on the front steps. I could hear her out there resting, her breath slowing as she leaned back in the shade. She rose a few moments later. At first I thought she was going to turn and go right back down the mountain without saying anything. Thinking this, I found myself wanting to call out to her. I think I probably would have if she hadn't suddenly turned and called to me, "Eddie!"

Somehow hearing her voice stilled my own. I ignored her.

"Please, Eddie, can't we just talk?"

I maintained my silence.

"*Eddie,*" she wailed. "Can't you just let things be. I told you I was sorry. What more can I do?"

"Leave me alone."

"I can't leave you alone."

"You could if you wanted."

"Well then, I don't want to," she said, and I figured we had talked enough.

"Eddie, just come out and sit with me for a while?" she said. When she realized it wasn't going to do any good, she ignored my silence and went right on. "My leg's been bothering me some. I figure next week I'll bring up extra stuff, just in case."

She waited.

I wanted to reply, I really did, but I couldn't get the words out. I couldn't ask her how she was feeling. The words were a mass of indigestible food stuck in my throat that tasted like dog.

"Eddie?" she called once more. Then, a few moments later, she gave up and began the trek back down the mountain.

I waited until she passed from sight before I went outside to pick up the supplies. I could sense her out there, somewhere at the ridge of the hill, watching, and I let her have her moment before I picked everything up and carried it into the cabin.

I waited a little while longer, then went outside and raced into the woods. I caught up with her a couple of hundred yards from the cabin and followed her, always keeping out of sight, watching, finding the memories of her more painful than I wanted them to be.

I want to hate her. She deserves it, but I can't. The only thing I can do is not speak to her. I know what this does to her, but I wonder if she has any idea of what it does to me. Probably not. The silly old fool never was very good at empathy.

Long after she had gone, I returned to the cabin and put the supplies away, forcing my thoughts from her onto Alovar. He's been giving me trouble. I've got him in the old city and dread what might happen next. I'm still not sure how to handle it. It scares me to attempt writing something like that.

Already, for the past three days, I've spent hours with him, attempting to get it down correctly, but so far I just can't seem to find the right emotions, or the motivation that will dictate his behavior.

Lying there this morning, thinking about Alovar and the old woman irritates me. I'm tired of both their problems and have begun to realize that a plot solution is becoming increasingly important. John was right: I can't keep avoiding the issue. Alovar can't go on forever the way he has. He has nothing. No tribe, no friends, just those he defends and those he conquers. He needs more than that to maintain his existence. If I don't provide him with more, I'm going to have to kill him. It's not fair of me to make him live the way he does.

In some ways, I think, his problems are similar to the old woman's. I'm not being fair to her either. It's been long enough, this silence I've maintained. What she did was horrendous and unforgettable, but it was forgivable. And in a way—a tangent of memory that I detest pursuing—the fault was more mine than hers. I was the one who lost control. The question that haunts me: was I acting out the role that everyone, even my biological father, had assigned me, or was I only coming closer to what I actually am?

These are not good thoughts to begin the day. I push myself out of bed in a huge burst of energy, then lurch over to the cook stove. After I set the water to boil and get the coffee ready, I race outside, around the cabin to the shower, and quickly wash myself off, shivering in the morning chill. After breakfast, sitting on the front porch watching the sun dapple the trees, the taste of cigarette smoke on my tongue and the warm flood of coffee in my mouth, I decide that the next time the old woman comes up, I'll talk to her. Maybe not a lot, but enough.

Deciding this makes me feel better. It suddenly brings a flood of memories that I've kept hidden for a long time: the old woman coming up to the attic, carrying a platter of food, sitting with me, watching me eat in my own inimitable way, never saying anything, just watching, content to watch me. The look on her face, a glance that I have never seen, and will probably never see, on any other face. Love.

Traveling across the country with her. Me out of control with the sudden, heady freedom, even if it was only an illusion, and she showing a patience toward me that I can only now appreciate.

The campsites we occupied. The moment of waking up to a new world filled with sights and scents that I had never before encountered, and that one moment of terror, and then the feel of her sleeping body beside me. The sound of her breath, her hand, as even in her sleep she sensed my unease and moved to still it.

Her long treks to the cabin with that first stupid red wagon trailing behind her, and my anticipation of her arrival.

The times I would stand impatiently pawing the ground, lifting my head in the air, trying to pick up her scent.

And then those other times, those times I waited and waited, watching the sun rise and set without her arrival. The slow realization that even she, this one poor old woman, who had always been the only person to had ever given me any sense of my own humanity, that she was ultimately also going to reject me.

The depression came long before the hunger and stayed long after the hunger had disappeared. No apology, no matter how abject, could ever take this away. It was a part of me and always would be.

Standing on the porch, realizing this, I can finally accept it. I have no other choice. I must simply accept it.

I go off and gather wood, storing it behind the cabin and along the porch for easy access when the snow begins to fall.

I lie across the porch, eating lunch, and I work on Alovar. I write pages and pages of notes, then rip them up, not sure how to begin.

I take to the woods. I crouch down at the base of Flag Mountain and smoke a cigarette, listening to the forest around me. I pick up scents: birds, squirrels, a fox. Heading home, I circle to the south, examining every step closely. I read the surrounding ground and shrub like a book. A feather with a bloodstained tip, a scraggle of claw marks, the darting print of a hawk as it swooped down upon a dove. A tree's wounded trunk. The hoof print of deer, hidden in the scramble of decaying leaves at the base of a birch tree. The sound of a crow dislodged from his perch by a jay. A squirrel's throaty clucking at his sudden discovery of a batch of hickory nuts. The screech of a magpie, the guttural call of a frog by the stream, the trout luxuriating in the cold water, and through all of this I think of the old woman and the things that I will say to her.

The leg's bad. The worst it's been. Last night I rubbed it down with alcohol, thinking that if I just took it easy, it might be all right today. It isn't. I think I knew that last night, but didn't want to admit it.

Is he going to think I've forgotten him again? Will he remember my mentioning about my leg?

I don't know what to do. I keep looking at it, thinking the swelling will go away if I keep wishing, but it still looks the same, all swole up, and that big red scar running down the front of the knee. When I see that scar, I remember the feel of it, that ax coming out of nowhere like a snake and biting into me, looking down right after it happened, seeing only this split pucker of flesh that seemed to go right to the bone. For one instant there was only the cut. Nothing else. The next moment there was this sudden flood of red that seemed to wash it all away.

I still couldn't believe he'd done it, couldn't believe he had that kind of thing in him. But looking up at him, seeing the way his teeth were, and knowing that he was going to do it again, I still couldn't bring myself to do anything to stop him. Watching the arc of the ax, seeing it go over his shoulder all in one motion, and knowing this time it was going to be worse, all I could do was scream, *"Eddie,"* and hope that he might hear, might know that even then I was thinking about him, that I still loved him.

I don't know what to do. He's up there and I know he's waiting for me. How much food does he have left? Did I bring him enough canned goods? Has he been saving up enough to get by on?

I have only enough coffee left for another day, then I'll have to start reusing the grounds. I've learned how to do this.

I count my cigarettes again and come up with the same total as last night. Snorting in irritation, I treat myself and smoke a whole one. I do this standing before the cupboard, checking my supply of canned goods. I have enough for a week if I ration carefully.

I think of all the times I meant to tell the old woman to bring up extra supplies and I growl in annoyance. I try not to think of her as I hunch down against the cabin wall on the porch, scratching the knobs of my spine as I spoon a can of beans. The beans are difficult to digest and leave me feeling gaseous and irritable. I try to wash the taste of them away with the last dregs of my coffee, but it doesn't seem to work. It follows me around for most of the morning.

I gather wood and stack it on the porch, finding myself stopping often to lift my head, trying to pick up her scent. It annoys me that I do this, and each time I promise myself not to do it again, but I can't help it.

I keep thinking of my decision, almost a week old, to speak to her again, and I growl in irritation at my servility. I will never speak to her again, I vow to the woods and the forest around. Then I quickly lift my head, thinking I've caught her scent, but it's only a patch of dandelions blooming for one last time before the first freeze sets in.

In the afternoon I try to work on Alovar, but he ignores me and won't let me in. Tearing up the pages, I try to bite back the anger that comes so readily. It overwhelms me and leaves me howling at the sky. A bank of clouds, far off to the west, as if responding to my cries, moves across the sun, darkening the cabin. I welcome the shadows as a reflection of my own grotesque image.

In the evening I turn on the radio and dance. I dance, leaping into the air until the very floorboards threaten to crack beneath my feet. Hours later, I crawl into bed and fall asleep to the smell of my own stale sweat.

I dream of nothing, only color, and the color is bright red and splashes in front of me in a huge gout of anger.

I wake the next morning, cursing the day I was born and the moronic old woman who bore me.

It's done. There was nothing else I could do. I hope Eddie understands. I hope he at least tries to understand. I know how crazy he gets, but he's got to see that I had to do this. What else was there? I couldn't leave him up there alone.

CHAPTER
7

LYING ON MY bed, weakened by lack of food, and having decided that I would not go out, I would sooner starve to death than do what I had done last time, I heard the approaching vehicle. It drew nearer and nearer, until it was at the foot of the path by the gate. Hearing the abrupt silence as the engine stopped, I leaped out of bed and raced towards the door.

Once outside, I rushed down the hill, torn between anger and relief that she had finally arrived. Halfway down the path I skidded to a halt, floundering on all fours in the dust as my nostrils picked up a strange scent. It took only a moment to disappear into the underbrush. This new smell, it was not the old woman, I realized, my nose twitching, snorting in huge gouts of air. The scent was sweeter, not as stale. Who was it?

It would not be the first time someone had threatened to trespass on my property. Despite the signs and barbed wire, there were always a few inconsiderate fools or arrogant sportsmen who walked right on obliviously. I usually made short work of them. Following them, keeping myself hidden until I felt the time was right, I would suddenly howl at the top of my lungs. Watching them scramble back down the hill, had always been a great source of amusement. But this scent was not like theirs.

Catching the aroma of a passing squirrel, I felt my stomach growl. A quick thump stilled its grumbling.

Keeping myself hidden, I waited to see who this could be. I heard the familiar noise of the wagon. It had to be she. Who else would have the wagon? But how could she have changed her scent so completely?

I kept to the brush, peering out at the crest of a small hill through the limbs of a pine tree.

Her hair appeared first. The sun shining fully down on the hill was suddenly split almost in two by the bright color of her hair. Orange with a dash of yellow down the center. The sight of this bizarre hair, cresting the hill, startled me.

A moment later her face appeared. This young woman had the old woman's wagon in tow.

The wagon was filled with supplies I could identify by both sight and scent: the sweet smells of cookies and tobacco, coffee, paper . . . What had happened to the old woman?

My rage at her over the last week had known no bounds. My earlier decision to reconcile with her had only infuriated me more. Seeing this other woman, realizing that something must be wrong, made me feel ashamed.

I turned silently and made my way back to the cabin, trying to figure out what was going on. By the time I reached it, I had decided that whatever had happened to the old woman could not be too serious, or else no one would have come up with my supplies. She must be well enough to convince someone to do this, I rationalized, then immediately wondered, what has she told them? This woman coming towards the cabin, what does she know know about me?

These questions, along with my hunger, made me frantic. I had to force the howl back down my throat, knowing it would have the young woman racing back down the path to her car.

I searched my cupboards, trying to find anything that might appease my increasingly disruptive stomach and came up with an old potato. I scraped off a few of the more obscene eyes and popped it into my mouth. Dripping potato juice down my chest, I leaned forward on the window ledge and stared out at the path.

Again I got to watch her slowly appear. It was like some religious ascension watching her step over the hill, in full view of the cabin for the first time. The sunlight was at its zenith, and the bright green of the pine trees around her only added to the vibrant color of her hair and the textures of her flesh.

The woman stopped a good thirty feet from my porch.

"My name's Katherine. Your mother asked me to bring these things up to you." She paused, waiting for me to respond.

When I didn't, she went on, a little more tentatively,

"She's okay. Her leg's all screwed up and it's going to take a week or two before she'll be able to get up here again." She paused again and stared curiously towards the cabin. Her gaze was so intense that I ducked even lower beneath the window. I felt as if her eyes were piercing the walls.

"Hey! Are you in there or what?" she called, moving a few steps closer.

I cowered beneath the windowsill, nostrils dilated, taking in every nuance of her scent, savoring it.

"Well, I'm going to put this stuff up on your porch," she called. The wagon wheels squeaked.

I peered out, examining her closely. She wore a pair of jeans, frayed at both knees—the flesh showed through. Very supple white flesh, I noticed.

"You going to help me with this junk or what?" she called. Silence. "You in there? Anybody . . . anybody home?"

I could only stare out at her, unable to believe I was this close. Only six feet separated us, just that and the flimsy wall of the log cabin.

She was silent again, her eyes examining the structure just as closely as I was examining her. What she did next horrified me.

She took a deep breath, then stepped up onto the porch. I knew immediately what she had in mind and, in a whirlwind of limbs and hair, I rushed to the door and quickly threw the bolt.

"I heard that!" she screamed triumphantly. "You're in there. Why won't you talk to me?"

Leaning against the bolted door, heart thumping like some insane rabbit, I could only shake my head in response.

I heard her footsteps on the planking and dove across the floor and underneath the bed. Curled up beneath it, I peered out through the fringe of the blanket as her face appeared first at one window then another.

Trembling, finding it difficult to breath, I was absolutely terrified of being discovered. Anyone who looks like I do should certainly not be cowering beneath the bed, for Christ's sake, I thought disgustedly. What kind of a man am I?

A moment later, when I heard her knocking at the far window, I had my answer. I gulped in terror and shifted even farther beneath the bed.

She circled the cabin slowly, tapping at windows and walls, until finally she came around to the porch again.

"I give up," she called. "You can hide if you want to."

Rather than making me feel relieved, this had a strange effect on me. I found that I was let down that her search had ended. In some esoteric way, I realized, I had been enjoying myself.

She resumed unpacking the bags and I shuffled over to the window again. Safely positioned at the lower corner of it, I watched, noticing the way her jeans tightened and relaxed across her butt. A sudden flurry of motion outside startled me. I ducked, but not quickly enough as she sang out, "I saw you!"

I huddled against the wall. I think she knew and made no further attempt to try the other windows. She just stood in front of the one. After a minute, she sighed and stepped away. I heard the sound of the bags being unpacked again.

"You know, I walked all the way up here to bring you food. It seems to me the least you could do is say something to me."

She paused, waiting for me to respond. It didn't seem to bother her when I didn't.

"Your mother's been pretty worried about you. She made me promise not to tell anyone about any of this." She turned, glancing coyly at the front of the cabin.

I could sense the way her mind was working. It was not a direction I was particularly pleased about. I remained silent.

"All right, all right, that was a lousy thing to say. I take it back. But you know, you could at least say hello or thank you."

I watched her bend over to pick up the last bag, my eyes intently focused on the momentarily elevated part of her anatomy.

Placing the last bag on the steps of the porch, she paused to stretch, then turning to glance at the path, she said, "It's nice up here. I like it." She sat down on the top step of the porch.

"I'm just going to rest for a moment and then I'll go, okay?" She didn't bother waiting for my response. "You should plant some flowers along here. That would look nice. Maybe some tulips. You put them in now, they'd bloom by spring. You need a little more color up here. It's all too brown and green. Those aren't great colors. They can cause depression if you're not careful. Sky helps a little bit. Blue's always good for bad days, but you need some reds here. You get depressed much, being up here all alone?"

Her question took me by surprise.

"I guess not, huh," she went on. "Well, people handle things differently. I don't think I could live up here this way. Be a great visit, but doing it permanently would be too much for me. I like people." She leaned back against the porch stoop.

She began to talk again, but I ignored her and moved swiftly over to the counter and grabbed my last cigarette. I had been saving it for my confrontation with the old woman. But now, smelling the fresh tobacco on the porch, I felt little need to continue to conserve. Quickly back at the window, I spit up a bit of potato and lighted up, inhaling the stale smoke.

"And then when my family told me I was coming here, I just about died. I mean who the hell in their right mind wants to go to Idaho. What's in Idaho? Just potatoes and Christians and both of them have too many eyes," she was saying, when I finally caught up with her conversation. The cigarette was making me mildly dizzy.

"You're a big smoker, I guess, huh? Never did it myself. Never liked the way it smelled. You ever smell someone who smokes a lot? I guess it's hard if you smoke yourself. But sometimes, when I'm around a heavy smoker, I think they smell just like death. It's an old greasy smell, like something that's yellow and's been left in a dark corner too long."

I snuffed my arm curiously. It didn't smell any different than it usually did.

"You think you're going to talk to me? I just wanted to know, because your mother wants me to do this again tomorrow. I'm preparing you, just in case you want some time to think about what you might say."

I listened to her, enjoying her voice, thinking how few I'd heard in my life and how different hers was from anyone else's. I suddenly realized why this was. It was because she was talking to me. Only the old woman, her husband, and now she, had ever spoken to me. He never talked to *me* but to the thing he thought I was, and the old woman always talked to me like a mother would talk to her son, but this woman outside, Katherine, she was talking to me like I was a person, just a normal everyday person.

This realization flooded me. For a moment it was so overwhelming that I had thrown back my head and was about to howl, before I remembered and stilled my voice. I crouched by the window, teeth bared in a fierce grin.

"I suppose I should start back," she said, rising to her feet and smoothing her jeans down over her thighs. I watched the way her hands moved along her legs, the tiny glint of golden hairs on her arms. I snorted, filling my nostrils, and took her scent deep into my lungs.

She turned, maybe having heard the noise, and stared curiously at the window.

"You're right there, aren't you?" she asked a bit nervously. "Watching me?"

Still hidden, I nodded.

"You know, it can't be that bad. I've seen burned people before. My cousin Howard burned his arm real bad on the kitchen stove once. It looked terrible but it didn't make him any different. It was still Howard under all those blisters, and later it was still Howard's arm beneath the scar."

I grunted softly.

She heard it, and before I could decide if I had wanted to be heard or not, she smiled. I bared my teeth back at her, but made sure that I remained hidden.

"That's our conversation for the day then, huh? I talk and you grunt." She nodded. "All right, if that's the way you want it. Maybe tomorrow you'll be feeling a little more talkative," she said, then stooped down to take up the handle of the wagon and began to wheel it away.

I watched her disappear over the hill. My last sight of her was her hair and the way the sun brightened its colors.

I wanted to rush out the door after her but forced myself to wait. Her scent was still strong and I knew what she was doing. It was not an unfamiliar trick.

Twenty minutes later I heard the faint sound of the wagon again and felt her scent recede.

I raced out the door, scooped up a bag of Oreo cookies, and was off into the woods. Mouth stuffed, noisily gulping air through my nostrils, I raced up the hill. I paused on the other side, where she had hidden herself, and glanced back towards the cabin. It gave a clear view of the front door. The matted grass was redolent with her scent. I inhaled deeply, then raced back into the woods and down towards the gate.

I caught up with her three-quarters of the way to the gate, and followed her the rest of the way down. She paused once to pick up a piece of quartz. She held it up to the sunlight, and for a moment the rays shafted through the thin fabric of her shirt. I could see the outline of her breasts, tightly molded beneath the heavier white of her brassiere. The sight made the hairs on the back of my neck and arms stand on end.

At the gate she unlocked the chain and pulled the wagon to the other side, then rechained it. Right before she climbed into her car, she turned and stared at the woods. It surprised me when she suddenly smiled. Then she turned and climbed into her car.

I stayed, listening to the sound of the engine until it slowly faded and disappeared. It left only the emptiness of the forest around me, which suddenly seemed extraordinarily loud.

I took my time going back and stopped again at the matted grass where she had hidden herself. I crouched down, inhaling her, then lowered myself into the same spot and rolled in it.

I went back to my cabin with her scent all over me. That night, burrowed beneath the tent of my blankets, I could still catch its subtle odor.

CHAPTER

8

I DON'T KNOW what to think. She said everything went fine, but it's the way she says it that makes me wonder. It's like she knows something that she isn't telling me. I kept wanting to tell her that this is serious, this isn't some parlor picture she can pick up and examine, this is someone's life, and if she isn't careful it could break apart. But before I could even start, Jake showed up.

He came over to see how I was doing. It was all I could do to talk to him, try to act like everything was just fine.

At one point he asked Kat where she'd been all day. When she turned to me and winked, I could feel my heart pounding in my chest.

"I was with Annie," Kat said, turning back to Jake.

He glanced over at me and smiled, then said, "Well, I'm glad the two of you are getting along so well."

We both smiled back at him. All the time I kept wishing he'd leave, so I could talk to Kat and try to find out what had happened, but he stayed, fussing around me like I was some kind of cripple.

The leg's still bad, but I can get around with the crutches

Doc Calken gave me. He came by earlier and told me a week or two and I should be just fine, so long as I don't overdo it. It's hard for me not to when I think about Eddie up there. It's even harder when I think about Kat going up there. I wonder if he talked to her. Way she was acting, it seemed like he might have. Hard for me to imagine that. Eddie's never talked to anybody but me and Ted.

Towards the end, when Ted got all crazy, Eddie hardly talked at all, even to me. It was like he knew what was going to happen, could smell it somehow. I tried to ask him about this once, but he would only look at me and shake his head, as if what he knew was too much for me to know. I hope he knows enough now not to do anything foolish.

Kat said she'd come by tomorrow morning to take the other load up to him. She sounded like she was looking for ward to it. Then Marilyn came by and there was no way I could get away from her. She sat right down across from me and every time I started to pick up my crutches, she'd say, "No, you just rest, I'll get it for you." Thing I wanted to get, was just away from her for a while to think some, but she seemed to sense this and wouldn't let me do it.

She stayed for a good two hours, talking about the church and how much it's done for her since Don died. I listened as polite as I could, knowing that she was just taking her time getting around to it.

"Annie? Why don't you come with me some Sunday?" she finally asked.

Looking across at her, seeing that she was just being nice, made me feel terrible about the way I'd been thinking about her. I know what she was feeling. There was a time in my own life when I'd felt the same way. The church helped me get through some pretty bad parts of my life, and for a long time I thanked God every night for his being there for me. But after Ted, and all that followed with Eddie, I realized that it was all just hocus-pocus. There wasn't anything out there but what we pretended was out there. And it seemed to me I was too old to be pretending that kind of thing. It was time to start taking up my life the way I should, rather than praying to the walls of my room, thinking they were going to help me somehow.

But how could I say this to Marilyn? She had the belief. And it wasn't a bad thing really, it was just something that wasn't there for me anymore.

"I just lost my belief," I said, looking away from her, like it was a hard thing for me to say.

"But Annie," she replied, coming over and sitting down beside me. "We all question our faith sometimes. It's just a matter of believing in the Lord."

"It's just not there anymore, Marilyn. I wished it was but it's gone."

"Maybe if you came back to the church, just for a week or two, it might come back."

I shook my head and told her I didn't think that was going to help any.

"But won't you try, Annie? Won't you try?" she said. "For me?"

"No. I can't."

It was a hard thing to say. But I wasn't going to do that for her or anyone else. Religion hadn't helped me any when I needed it, and it seemed stupid to think that, now that I didn't need it, I could go back to pretending it could.

I never told Ted, and I never told Eddie, but when I first knew he was coming, I went up to the hospital in Cumberland. Ted was off working or something, so I just drove myself up there in the Nova. I wanted to surprise Ted. I wanted to come

back and tell him that we could just be thinking about boys'
names and not bothering about the girls. They had that test
that'd tell you what kind of baby you were going to have, and I
just had to know.

I didn't know why it was so important to me then. I knew
Ted wanted to have a boy and I guess I just thought I'd find out
a little sooner, to kind of prepare myself. But now, when I
think about it, I think I knew something wasn't right, that
whatever was growing in me was different.

The doctor took me right into the examining room and
had me lie down on this table all covered with that crinkly
white paper. He put this thing on my stomach and started to
slowly move it around until he suddenly stopped and said,
"There he is."

I remember I smiled when I heard "he," thinking how
pleased Ted would be and what a good idea this all was. I was
already thinking about the drive home and how hard it was
going to be, waiting for Ted to get back to tell him the news. I
knew he'd be happy. Wouldn't have mattered to him if it was a
boy or a girl, he was always saying, but I knew.

"Can I see him?" I asked, trying to twist around to see the
screen.

"Just lie quietly for a moment longer, Mrs. Talbot," the
doctor said, and I could hear it in his voice.

"What's wrong?"

"Just a moment," he said again, then leaned forward to
stare at the screen. He looked at it for a long time.

I twisted around to see it, but he turned it off before I
could.

"What is it?" I asked again, looking up at him, seeing it in
his face, but not knowing exactly what it was. "What's wrong?
Is my baby all right?"

He glanced away, then a few moments later turned back to me. "I think we should run a few more tests."

"What, what's wrong?"

"It's too soon to be sure and I don't want to—"

"What, what is it!" And this time I wasn't asking. It took him a moment to answer, and when he did his words seemed to come out so softly that I had to lean all the way forward just to make them out.

"The baby hasn't fully developed through the first trimester," he said, looking at me closely. I think he was hoping that I would understand without his having to say anything more.

"What d'you mean?"

"During pregnancy, a child goes through various stages of development. Each stage reflects in some way the evolutionary process. Your child, Mrs. Talbot, appears to be unable to grow through each of these stages."

"He's deformed. You're saying he's going to be deformed?" I asked, sitting up now, staring at him, trying to understand this thing he was telling me.

"Yes, I am. I'm sorry. We can run some more tests but I don't think it's going to show anything different," he said, then paused and added, "There are things we can do, Mrs. Talbot. There are options. You're a young woman and you'll have many other opportunities to bear children."

"You mean abortion, don't you?"

"Yes."

I drove home blindly—half-dazed.

There was no one to talk to about this. I couldn't tell Ted; I knew what it would do to him. He'd been so happy, and the thought of bursting that joy didn't seem fair to me, at least until I figured out what it was I wanted to do.

How abnormal? I kept wondering. Would he have an extra finger or something? I could live with that. Or would it be something worse?

I remembered seeing pictures of those babies back in the fifties whose mothers were taking that medicine. Some of those babies were born without any arms or legs. Could mine be like that?

I talked to the only person I could think to talk to. Reverend Lynch.

"Are you sure, Annie? Are you absolutely positive the baby will be this way?"

Crying, unable to stop the tears, I could only nod my head.

"It's a hard thing, something like this," the Reverend said, leaning back in his chair. "But the Lord sometimes sets a hard path for those He thinks can manage it. It's not for us to choose. We just follow His plan. But you know all this, don't you?" he asked gently.

"Yes," I nodded, knowing that all I wanted was to speak to someone, to say the words out loud and hear them.

"Is it Ted?"

"I don't know what to do. I don't know how to tell him."

"Annie," he said, leaning forward to take my hand in his. "I can't tell you what to do. I can only tell you to follow your own heart. You're a good woman. You know what's right. And what's right, Annie, isn't always what's easiest."

I left feeling easier. He was a good man, I thought, and his words calmed me. I went home and tried to think of some way to tell Ted. It was only right that he should know.

I spent the next four months trying to think of some way to say those words. I never did come up with them. And after

Eddie was born, the way Ted started acting, there was no way I could ever tell him about my having known ahead of time.

He died, not knowing that I knew about Eddie long before he was born. I think now it wouldn't have made much difference. The bad in Ted was there and would have come out one way or another. The evil in Reverend Lynch was also there, only I was too stupid to see it. I believed everything he had told me. He was a man of God, how could I not believe him? But God's only what you want Him to be. People all over the world think He's one thing or another, and a lot of times what they believe doesn't have a whole lot to do with what He might really be.

"No!" the Reverend shouted, glaring at me across the kitchen table, with Ted standing right beside him.

"Why not?"

"You want me to baptize *that*—that thing up there?"

"He's my son."

"That thing isn't even human. To baptize something like that is blasphemous. The church will have nothing to do with this," the Reverend said, rising from his chair, glaring at me, accusing me.

I looked to Ted, waiting for him to say something, but he just calmly leaned back against the door frame with a cigarette between his lips.

I said, "Reverend, please. He's my son, he's only an infant."

"That is no infant, Annie Talbot. That is a judgment on the sinfulness and error of your ways. Get down on your knees and beg forgiveness, then rid yourself of that spawn." The Reverend leaned forward to take my hand. "It's not God but

Satan that has given you this offspring. Rid yourself of it and come back into the arms of the church."

I jerked my hand away from him and stood. "Get out of my house."

"Annie!" he said.

"Get out. I don't want you or your miserable church anywhere near me or my son."

"Annie Talbot, I understand what you're going through, but think about what you're saying. God is all forgiving but there are some—"

"Get *out!*" I shouted at him, moving around the table towards him, not quite sure what I was going to do, but knowing, if I got my hands on him, I'd do something.

After he left, I sat back at the table. When I glanced up again, Ted was still standing in the doorway, looking at me, the cigarette between his lips.

"What?" I asked.

He simply turned and walked out of the room. Never said a word.

Reverend Lynch never did say anything again about Eddie, which I guess is something I should be thankful for. It's the one thing he did that I could at least call Christian-like, but I think it was more for his own sake than for me or Eddie. I believe he was ashamed of himself. Not for refusing Eddie; rather, ashamed that he had all but told me to have the baby.

Marilyn left after a while. She said she'd check in on me again, but I could tell she was disappointed that I wouldn't go to church with her. There was no way to explain exactly how I felt. It's all just words. The words don't mean anything anymore. Maybe they did once, but now people just say them and then turn around and do something hateful or spiteful. And

God, if he's up there, just lets them go right on like this. He never shows them any different. It's like as long as no one bothers him, he's not going to bother anyone else.

I once read in the paper about some folks down in Mexico who cooked a tortilla that had an image of Jesus Christ on it. They just cooked it and it came out like that. They claimed it was a miracle. If all God's worried about is some folk's tortilla, then he sure isn't anyone I want interfering in my life or Eddie's.

Eddie has no belief. He told me once he believes only in what he can see, touch, or smell, and even that, he said, sometimes isn't right.

When he was eight he asked me about God and religion, and I thought about it a long time before I decided I'd tell him about it but wouldn't let him know how I felt. I figured he should at least have the chance to believe if he wanted.

When I was done, Eddie just looked at me with his face all furrowed and asked me how far away heaven was.

"No one knows," I told him. "You only get to go there when you die."

"But if you're dead, then how can you tell anybody that it's there?"

"Well, no one ever has exactly."

"Then how do you know it's there?"

"'Cause that's what the Bible tells us."

"The Bible's just a book. How'd you know that the man who wrote it was telling the truth?"

"Because the Bible tells us it's the truth."

"Nobody really believes that, do they?" he asked.

Doc Calken says another two weeks before I should even think about getting around again. It's going to take at least another trip to get Eddie stocked up again. Can she do that? Will she do that?

My leg aches and I'm so tired but I can't sleep. I keep thinking of all the things, the bad things, that could happen.

All this pain, it seems like everything now is just pain. I wish it would all go away. How can anyone believe in anything when there's so much pain to account for?

CHAPTER
9

FOR A WEEK Alovar explored the ruined city, and always during these explorations he felt, in some vague manner, as if he were being watched. There was nothing tangible. It was an instinct that Alovar had acquired in his years of wandering the Wasteland.

He used every tactic to discover this unseen observer, but none was fruitful. Finally, he decided that it was the city itself that watched him. It was the vacant eyes of the buildings atop the broken mouths of doorways that made him so uncomfortable.

He continued his explorations, finding things that defied all explanation. One of these was a small metal box that had two blackened slits in the top. When Alovar thrust his knife into one of the slits, it would give slightly, then suddenly the blade would catch on something inside. He would withdraw his knife and wait. A few moments later there would be a bouncing noise.

Alovar, who had walked away a few feet, whirled around, sword in hand. The noise, he realized, had come from the box. He experimented with it. Soon he found that, by putting small pieces of wood in the metal thing, it would pause for a moment, then spit the wood out into the air. He found this object amusing and tried putting heavier things inside. It was good with wood, but metal and stone seemed too heavy for it.

Alovar kept this metal thing by his campfire at night and tinkered with it, trying to discover its secrets.

In one of the buildings he found a huge stack of paper books. He carried the books back with him to his campfire and pored over them for most of the day. The pages of these books were filled with drawings of people so beautiful and unmarked by the world that Alovar began to wonder if they had ever been real, these people and their wondrous inventions: air machines, land machines, and strange, complicated things that they used on their bodies. None of this made sense to Alovar. He spent the whole day trying to reach some understanding of the pages.

He discovered that the scribbles across the front of the paper books were sometimes similar. Squinting, he carefully sifted through, stacking the ones with the same scribbles in separate piles. When he was done he had four piles. Three of them had almost three hand counts of books, the fourth had only half a hand.

He paged through each pile carefully, trying to understand them. He discovered that one pile of books always showed women. The women in these books were beautiful beyond any of the other books.

Another of the piles had things and people in them. The people in these books were not always beautiful. Some of them were wounded or even dead. These pictures Alovar examined closely, trying to understand why anyone would draw pictures like this. There were even children in these books. Some of the children looked long unfed and had tears and insects in their eyes. Looking at them, Alovar would glance at the other pile of books, the beautiful women books, and he'd try to understand how they could both exist. Didn't the beautiful women know of these children? And if they did, how could their beauty be so undiminished? Lost in such thoughts, Alovar found himself pondering the Realm and life inside its boundaries. Wasn't it much the same there? The mutant and Marauders subsisted out in the Wasteland, while those untouched by the light lived so well inside the Realm.

Alovar leaned back from his fire, the book open on his lap, and tried to understand that which was so different yet still the same.

The third pile had nothing but machines. Huge machines that seemed to fill the pages with their hard metal. Many of them Alovar could not fathom. He could not discover their use. But some of them, the smaller ones, seemed to be for carrying people and things. Their bright colors hypnotized him. He couldn't believe machines could be so beautiful. In one of the pictures there was a beautiful woman standing beside a machine, the woman's beauty reflected off the very surface of the machine. He returned to this picture often, until soon it became creased and wrinkled from his examinations.

In the final pile, the one with the fewest paper books, were pictures that at first Alovar didn't understand. He paged through these quickly, unable to comprehend the use of these things drawn across the pages. He discerned that they were made to be carried. This he could tell by the grips built and smoothed for hands, but what these things did he could not decipher.

A thought suddenly occurred to him about these pictures. He hurried to open one of the paper books, studied the objects closely, then picked up one of the paper books from the other pile. He opened this book and paged through it quickly until he came to the picture he had remembered.

It was by looking at both these pictures that he divined the use of the things in this last pile of paper books.

A man stood holding a long metal stick. The stick was hollowed out at one end and pointed towards another group of men. These men were all dressed the same and seemed weary and dirty. One of them had fallen to the ground. Across his chest was a huge splash of blood. The man holding the stick was smiling at the others still standing in front of him.

Another drawing was of the long metal sticks. Comparing the two of them, Alovar sensed it was a weapon, a thing that pushed objects from the mouth of the stick into other people's bodies.

With this discovery, Alovar once again pored over the whole pile of paper books, and this time he found meaning in the pictures. An explanation that enabled him to begin to understand these beautiful people. They were at war, and judging by the number of pictures, and the different colors of the people dying and holding metal sticks, they were at war with everyone. Alovar wondered if their women warred too.

Trying to find an answer to this, he leafed through his pile of books once more and found that the women were also pictured holding the metal weapons, only some of these were smaller than those brandished by the men. He found pictures where even children held these smaller weapons pointed at people. Having discovered what these things were, he concluded that one pile of books was filled with pictures of war.

It seemed everyone fought everyone with these strange weapons. Alovar found the weapons contemptible. Even a child could manage one. What pride could there be in conquering with such a thing, a thing that even a babe could wield? Alovar snorted in disgust, thinking the face of beauty was not a window but a wall.

After this, Alovar found the books not as amusing as he once had. Now he saw only the bodies splayed across various landscapes, twisted in grotesque death. These images were often interspersed with pages of the beautiful. He now found their faces offensive and cold and, looking at them closely, he discovered a similarity in their expressions with those among whom he had lived in the Realm.

He spent more time in the ruins and still always felt watched. He ignored it and continued to search out more about these ancient people.

In many of their buildings were drawings. Some were aged and half destroyed by vandals, but some were still intact. He found a drawing of a horse, so lifelike that he put his hand on the hindquarters almost expecting warmth and the coarse texture of the hide.

The horse was as perfect as all the beings who had occupied this city. Its back was unbowed and its legs were firm and unbroken. Not at all like the creatures that were used in the Realm.

There were many pictures of animals that Alovar had never seen before. Huge animals that he came to suspect must have existed long ago. He often wondered if any of these creatures were still alive. Could they have survived all the years of war these people waged? If they had, where were they hidden?

In all his years of travels through the Wasteland, he had never heard tell of anything like these beasts. Most of the remaining animals had been butchered for food. It was only inside the boundaries of the Realm that this was forbidden. And even there, during famine, an animal was occasionally sacrificed for a great celebration.

So the time passed for Alovar. He spent his days in exploration and his evenings studying the ancient paper books, trying to discover more of these people who were at once so handsome and so destructive.

His reserves ran low and he knew that soon he would be forced to retreat across the burnt lands to reprovision.

On the night before he had decided to begin his return journey, he felt the eyes again. At first he tried to ignore it, having convinced himself that it was only the city, but bowed over his paper book, he found the sensation too strong.

Not giving the faintest hint of this, he rose, stretched, then stepped from the light of the fire as if to relieve himself. Once in the surrounding darkness, Alovar crouched and moved quickly through the shadows to the side of a building. Standing there, he waited for his eyes to adjust to the dark. Soon he could make out the looming structures around him. Turning his head slowly, he let his eyes pry into the blackness, searching for the faintest movement. Nothing. As always, he thought, shrugging at his foolishness.

Then—motion. The barest trace. He froze in place. He made no attempt even to turn his head towards the movement. He stood like a part of the building alongside him. His sword was by the fire but his knife was in his belt. It would be enough, he thought. If it wasn't, then it wasn't.

The movement again—a sudden shifting of shadows. So subtle.

Alovar moved with the same stealth. Lowering himself slowly to the ground, he crept along the base of the building.

It came again, this time circling his campsite in the direction opposite from that he was moving in. Alovar understood. The watcher was trying to locate him. He knew that he would have to move quickly before whoever was out there realized that things were not as they appeared.

Alovar moved faster, risking his concealment for speed, thinking the watcher would be concentrating on his exit point from the campfire.

He circled warily, his eyes averted from its flame. The other's movements were soundless. He found it difficult to follow this shadow.

Alovar crouched in a doorway and searched. It took a moment before Alovar was even aware of the sound. It was so ordinary that he nearly dismissed it. But listening closely, examining the darkness ahead, he finally sensed what it was—another's breath.

There, only a few feet away, sprawled across the sand was a shadow without an object to cast it.

Alovar examined it, unable even to discern head from foot. He had no sense of its size or weight but knew that he must move quickly. It would be only moments before the watcher realized.

Alovar moved soundlessly towards his prey. Even so, the figure before him seemed to sense him, for he turned and attempted to rise to meet Alovar's onslaught.

Alovar fell upon the shadowy form and bore him down to the sand. They wrestled, turning from side to side, before Alovar's great strength subdued the other.

Twisting and spitting, the observer fought his grip and Alovar's legs around his waist. Alovar drove his fist into the face that he could only dimly feel in the darkness.

The observer slackened beneath him.

Cautiously Alovar disengaged himself. He kept his hand on the hilt of his knife, prepared to use it if needed, but the figure before him lay unmoving.

He grabbed and dragged the limp body back to the fire, and crouched down to examine this solitary watcher who had so skillfully stalked him for a week.

He yanked back the hood that covered the head, then recoiled in amazement at the face.

A woman lay before him. Her only blemish was the darkening bruise from his blow.

He knelt beside her, touching her lightly, in disbelief that she could actually exist. He remembered the strength in her struggle and the craft with which she circled his camp, and was amazed.

He opened her robe and looked at her body, finding it full and whole without any sign of the light. Both of her hands were well shaped and carried no mark of deformity.

Alovar sat back on his heels and considered this. He knew that the mutants sometimes carried deformities that were not always to be seen, and he felt that surely she must be one of these. He had never before encountered anyone, other than himself and those in the Realm, who was as unblemished as this female.

He covered her, then stepped back to the fire. He made tea and had just sat down to drink when the woman revived.

She came awake suddenly with no apparent confusion. One moment she was on the ground and the next she was on her feet, crouched, her hand buried beneath her robe.

Alovar, surprised by the abruptness of her actions, made no move. He simply glanced her way, then back to the far side of the fire where he had placed a mug of steaming tea. The woman followed his gaze, then looked at him closely.

"Who are you and what do you want?" she said.

Alovar found the question surprising. It seemed to be one that he should be voicing.

He asked softly, "Who are you and what do you want?" and sipped his tea.

The woman watched, her hand still beneath her robe.

"It's only tea, made from mulberry," Alovar said, nodding toward the other cup.

The woman took a tentative step towards it, never taking her eyes from him.

Alovar lifted his cup, watching just as closely. As he took a sip, she suddenly disappeared into the shadows.

Alovar continued sipping, making no effort to rise or pursue. He waited.

"What are you doing here?" Her voice came from somewhere behind him.

Alovar felt the hairs on his neck rising, but made no effort to turn.

"Exploring," he replied, his hands around the mug. He listened and heard her, and knew the sounds he was hearing were only those she was allowing him to hear.

He felt her behind him, then felt her grow even closer. Again he heard the sound of her breath and waited.

Her hands came around his neck. One held a knife. She turned the blade against his flesh and hissed, "I can gut you in an instant. What do you want here?"

"To see."

"There's nothing to see, only the waste."

"Then that is what I want to see."

"Why?"

Alovar shrugged, and felt the prick of the knife pierce his skin. "Why not?"

"Who are you? You're not a Marauder, and your features are clean. That makes you something different, something dangerous, I think," she said, leaning forward, bringing her mouth almost to his ear.

"And you," Alovar said, "what are you?"

"Your death," she whispered, and then the knife disappeared. Alovar listened closely, but she faded silently into the darkness.

He finished his tea then spread his blanket across the ground and prepared to sleep. He could still sense her out there, could feel her watching. It was a long time before sleep came, and even then she remained, examining him, trying to decide what he was.

In the morning, when he rose, he found a can of food placed by the side of his fire.

He opened it carefully and examined it. It was a substance he had never before seen or tasted. It was both sweet and tart at the same time. He ate it, fishing the small bits of it out with his knife, savoring each. When he was done he drank the juice and used his finger to scoop what he had missed.

CHAPTER
10

I WAKE TO the silence of the cabin around me. I growl, grunt, yawn hugely beneath my blankets, then smile, baring my teeth at the sunlight dripping through my windows.

I hum an old tune by the Dead Kennedys as I start up the wood stove and put the water on to boil.

Beneath the shower, with the cold chill of the morning seeping into my bones, I sing. My voice growls from beneath the cascading water and frightens away every creature within a mile of the cabin. It doesn't bother me this morning that this is so. It even incites me to sing louder. I finish the chorus with a flourish and stepped out from beneath the shower, stretching sleep tightened muscles.

I dry myself off on the front porch, looking out at the forest around me, smiling at it, wondering if she will really come again.

Over coffee and fresh doughnuts, I find myself, amazingly enough, thinking life is good. It's a curious thought for me, and one that stops me for a moment, but I find I feel too good to contemplate the why of it. Just feeling it is enough.

Rinsing the dishes, glancing at my fully stocked larder, I feel rich, fat, and glossy.

I step out onto the porch for my first cigarette of the day. As I inhale the fragrant smoke, I casually run a brush through my hair. I comb out my chest and arms until the hair is sleek and golden. I use a mirror to examine myself and am pleased with my image. Feeling I look quite good, I step back into the cabin, passing Alovar lying on my work desk. I wink at him, thinking how soon his fortunes will change.

Crouched against the wall of the cabin, I watch the sun begin to cut its way into the forest in front of me. I watch the way each leaf is slowly revealed in varying shades of moribund fall colors. I inhale deeply, taking in the scent of the forest around me, holding it until it threatens to burst right out of my chest with its sweetness.

I smoke another cigarette, absently smoothing down the hair on my chest, enjoying the silky feel of it. I find a name drifting on my tongue. I savor it, tasting it fully before I whisper it softly to the walls of my cabin.

"Katherine," I say, then say it again more slowly, bringing it out one syllable at a time until each of them sounds like a separate name. I smile hugely, feeling the clean bite of my teeth against my lips.

Puttering around the stove, I put together breakfast, anxiously glancing towards the window, head up, trying to sift through the normal morning noises for that one sound that will change everything.

I carried my oatmeal out onto the porch and ate it slowly, having chosen it because I could eat it so silently. It didn't intrude on hearing.

I spent an inordinate amount of time combing myself

some more, making sure that each hair was in place. And still she hadn't arrived.

I meticulously cleaned my cabin, sweeping in places I hadn't even seen before. Why was I doing all this? I knew I would never allow her to come inside, and the thought of her actually seeing me was completely out of the question. So why was I grooming myself and the cabin with such care? I had no answer, I just kept doing it.

Mid-morning and I was sitting on the front steps of my porch, wondering if I had time for yet one more shower, when I heard the distant sound of her car. One moment I was sitting and the next I was on my feet, prancing around my yard like a madman.

I waited until I heard the engine die before I raced off into the woods and down towards the gate. I negotiated the woods carefully, trying not to pick up too many burrs on my sleekly groomed self.

In the overhang of a pine tree I stopped to watch her unload the wagon and the groceries. She wore a tie-dyed shirt and a pair of baggy khaki pants. The pants disappointed me. I liked the other ones much better.

I followed her, making sure to keep myself hidden. At one point, she paused and turned to examine the woods. Her eyes passed right over me, thrilling me, and for just a moment, I thought about stepping out onto the path to announce my presence. Fortunately good sense overrode this fantasy. I raced back up to the cabin.

When she finally appeared on the crest of the hill, I was already comfortably ensconced inside beneath the window ledge to watch her descent.

"Oh, that's nice," was the first thing she said.

I grinned, knowing exactly what she was talking about.

"You put those up pretty quickly, didn't you?" she said, in a teasing tone of voice.

I grinned even wider, displaying every tooth in a largely dentated mouth.

She stepped up to the porch and stared at the window and curtains I had hung yesterday evening. I was quite pleased with them. Maybe they weren't made of the most aesthetic of fabrics but they served their purpose quite well. No one could look inside now unless they were opened.

She stood for a moment looking at the curtains, then with a shrug she turned back to the wagon and began to unload.

I was disappointed. Didn't she want to talk? What had I said to offend her?

She put the last bag on the porch, then arched her spine, rubbing one fist in the small of her back. I found the gesture absolutely charming.

"I put some stuff in there I thought you might like. There's some tulip bulbs and a can of mandarin oranges. I bought both of them with my own money," she said, and waited.

Mandarin oranges?

"All right," she said, then nodded, picked up the handle of the wagon, and began to walk away.

I couldn't believe it. How could she do this to me? She was going to leave.

I watched her start up the hill, expecting some kind of trap, but when she reached the top and slowly disappeared from sight, I began to think that maybe she really was going to leave.

I threw back my head and snorted, trying to pick up her scent. I expected it to be right there before me, much like yesterday when she had attempted to catch sight of me. But it was gone and, worse yet, it was rapidly fading.

I raced outside and into the forest. Quickly I caught up and kept myself hidden in the woods, paralleling her progress. I couldn't believe she was going to do this.

I followed her all the way to the gate. There she again paused to scan the woods, then pulled the key from her pocket and picked up the chain.

What else could I do?

"*Wait,*" I yelled, and when she turned back to the woods and smiled, I knew it had only been another ruse.

"Come on out," she called.

"I can't."

"I'll leave," she threatened.

"Then you'll just have to leave, because I can't come out. But I'll tell you what I can do," I added hastily.

"What?"

"Come back to the cabin and we can talk."

"Okay," she quickly agreed.

I turned and ran back through the woods and into the cabin. By the time she appeared, I had pulled most of the burrs from my chest and arms and was beside the window smoking a cigarette.

"Are you in there?" she asked breathlessly.

"Yes."

"Jesus, you're fast."

"I ran."

"So did I," she said, slumping down on the front step.

"I was faster."

"I don't know if that's the right word."

"What is?"

"How far is it to the gate?"

"About five acres to the gate, four hundred and eighty four yards per acre. Two thousand, four hundred and twenty total yards; a mile's one thousand, seven hundred, sixty. A little over a mile and a quarter."

"You just figure that out in your head?"

"Yes," I answered, looking at her on the porch, noticing the way her breasts seemed to jut out when she leaned back.

She shook her head, then shuffled around so that she faced my window. For a moment I cowered below it, then realized that I was safely hidden behind the curtain.

"So," she said a moment later, "what's happening?"

Looking at her sitting out there I could feel something most definitely happening, but decided it would be ungallant of me to mention it.

She waited a moment for me to respond. When I didn't, she cast an annoyed glance in my direction, then said, "You know you were supposed to talk. That's why I came back up here."

"I'm not very good at this," I answered honestly. "I haven't had much practice."

"Well, you should get some in while I'm here. How do you like it up here, let's start with that."

"I like it," I nodded, as I lighted another cigarette.

"That's not a good beginning," she informed me. "How long have you been living up here?"

"Eight years."

"You're kidding!"

"No."

"You've been up here *eight* years, all by yourself?"

"Yes."

"No wonder you don't know how to talk."

This struck me as being ridiculous. I felt I was doing quite well.

"You've only talked to your mother all that time?"

Ah, a trick question, I thought, and answered, "Sometimes."

"But not all the time?"

"No, not recently."

"Why not?"

"We had a falling-out."

"Now that's interesting. What happened?"

"I'd rather not say."

She glared at my window.

"It's personal," I explained, not quite sure about that description, but it seemed to satisfy her for the moment, though I had a feeling we might get back to it later. Katherine, I was beginning to learn, was not one to let much get by her.

"So you only talk to her *sometimes?*"

"Yes."

"How long ago was the last time?"

"Almost a year now."

She turned to stare at my window, "You haven't talked to your mother in a year?"

"Yes," I said, feeling strangely defensive.

"Your mother comes up every week with bags and bags of groceries for you and you don't even say hello to her?"

"Well, I usually say something to her."

"Like what?"

"I don't know," I shrugged, not quite able to remember much of anything, other than the usual bits of obscenity I would hurl at her.

"Do you come outside to see her?"

"Not in a while."

"In a year?"

"Yes, that would be about right."

"Does she talk to you?"

"She tries."

"What does she say?"

"She usually asks me to talk to her."

"But you don't?"

"No."

"Jesus," Katherine said, shaking her head in exasperation.

I waited for her to go on, thinking this was kind of fun. When she didn't, I said, "Don't you have any more questions?"

"You know," she shot back, rising to her feet and turning to stare at my window with her hands on her hips. "A conversation is not one person asking questions while the other one answers them. That's an interview. A conversation is two people conversing, exchanging ideas and observations."

"Yes," I said, agreeing in principle. That accomplished, she launched into a brief summary of her life to date.

"Well, they didn't know what to do with me. I mean, there they are, these two perfectly respectable people with a daughter that they think hates them. They never asked me about it. If they had I could have told them that I didn't hate them, I just hated what they were doing. I mean, Edward,"—she said, it again!—"they voted for Reagan not just once, but twice. How can you talk to people like that?"

There was an expectant pause, one that—I was beginning to learn—was mine to fill.

"I don't know much about politics," I said. "It doesn't seem to affect me one way or another."

"That's not true," Katherine said immediately, rising to

her feet. "It affects every person in the country. This country's yours, and if you don't take an interest in it, how can you expect it to take an interest in you?" She was glaring at my window.

How could I tell her that legally I wasn't even a person, that I didn't even exist? There was no birth certificate chronicling my advent, there wasn't anyone left who knew I was alive except her and the old woman, and sometimes I had found myself wondering about the old woman.

"Do you vote?"

"No."

"I want you to vote in the next election."

"Okay."

"That was too easy. Are you registered?" she asked. My easy acquiescence had made her suspicious.

"Yes," I answered, the first of the many lies I would tell her. I could sense she didn't quite accept this one, but she realized that there was very little she could do about it.

She sat back down, nudging one of the grocery bags with her foot. "Don't you want to bring this stuff inside?"

"I can do it later."

"I could help you put them away."

"That's all right, I don't mind. I'm used to it."

"Look at that," she said suddenly, pointing off to the west.

I peered out the window.

"Don't you see it, that cloud there, right above that one pine tree."

I followed her pointing arm but got stuck somewhere around her wrist, admiring the line of it and the golden hairs.

"That's the best one I've seen today. It looks a little like a Porsche. My best friend, Megan, has a Porsche. It's a black convertible. You know, the kind with the optional sun-roof.

We used to take it out at night and drive all around Rodeo Drive and Beverly Hills, pretending we were rich. All the tourists used to stare at us, thinking we were somebody." She suddenly giggled.

The sound of it made the hair on my chest and arms stand on end.

"I remember once Megan even signed an autograph. She signed Winona Ryder's name, and she doesn't look a bit like her. I couldn't believe she did that."

Not having the faintest idea who Winona Ryder was, I grunted.

"You know you do that a lot."

"What?"

"Grunt."

"I'm sorry."

"Don't be sorry, just don't do it, okay? It's annoying."

I grunted without thinking and was rewarded with her laughter.

"So what do you do up here all day?"

"I write."

"What do you write?" she asked, turning to face me.

I looked out at her sitting there with her arms wrapped around her knees. Her legs were slightly splayed and the deep shadows of her thighs kept trapping my gaze.

"What do you write?" she asked again.

"Books."

"Really?"

"Yes."

"What kind?"

"Science fiction."

"Have you ever been published?"

"Oh yes."

"C'mon, *really?*"

"Yes. I've had seven books published."

"You've had *seven* books published," she repeated incredulously, leaning forward to stare intently at the window. Her disbelief confused me. "Yes, seven," I said.

"What books?"

"The Alovar series."

"You're telling me that you're that Alovar guy?"

"Yes."

"But they're written by a woman."

"Yes, Annie Talbot."

"Your mother," she said softly, suddenly awed.

"Yes."

"Why would you do it that way?"

"Taxes," I answered casually, hoping she wouldn't pursue it further.

"I don't believe you wrote them."

"It's true," I shrugged.

"Prove it," she said skeptically.

"How?"

"Quick, what's the name of all the books?"

"*Alovar, The Exile, Wanderer, Wasteland, The Circle of the Realm,* and *Sanctuary.*"

"You *are* her, aren't you?"

"Yes."

"Megan read all of them. She was always telling me I should, too."

"You never read any of them?"

"No, I never did. I hate science fiction. It always seemed so phony to me." She paused, looking thoughtful. "Maybe I'll try one now. Be interesting . . . reading something written by somebody I know."

"I've got one you could borrow," I said without thinking.

"Okay, let's have it."

And there was the problem. "I'll give it to you before you leave."

She grinned, knowing exactly what that meant.

The sun was beginning to dip into the pines. She glanced away and said, "How bad?"

"How bad what?"

"How badly are you hurt?"

For a moment I had no idea what she was referring to.

"The accident— How badly were you burned?"

"Very bad."

"So bad that you don't think I could ever see you?"

"Yes."

"Why? I mean, we kind of know each other now. What difference would it make? People aren't what they appear to be. They're what's inside of them. That was the whole problem with my parents. They seemed to think that all that counted was what you wore, what you drove, and where you lived. It was like being around a TV commercial all the time. Everything always had to be so perfect. It made me want to vomit. Who cares about that stuff. Sometimes I think ugly might be the only real beauty there is. It's honest. It doesn't have any phoniness about it. It's right there before you and you can't ignore it. You either accept it or walk away from it, but you can't ever pretend that it isn't there." She said all this vehemently, then suddenly stopped.

I had listened, unable to comment, wishing I could believe this but knowing that I couldn't. Glancing down at my hirsute body, twisted into knobs and angles that defied all sense of humanity, I wished, more than I had ever wished for anything before, that what she had just said was true. But of course it wasn't. People were driven by the ideal of perfection. It never occurred to them that perfection was only an aspiration, and could never be tolerated as a reality.

"Will you let me see you?" she asked softly.

"No," I grunted.

"Please?"

"Katherine," I said, letting her name roll along my tongue, enjoying its length. "I can't."

"Maybe sometime?"

"Perhaps," I answered, in another of my lies.

She nodded, accepting this and rose to her feet. "I have to go now. Will you walk me down?"

"I would like that," I said, and she smiled. I tasted the smile for a moment longer before I said, "You go ahead. I'll be in the woods, beside you."

She nodded, then picking up the handle of the wagon, began to walk up the knoll.

I slipped soundlessly through the door of the cabin and into the woods before she crested the hill. I caught up with her on the other side.

"Are you there?" she said as she walked.

"Yes." I was only three feet from her beneath the overhang of a ponderosa.

"I feel better with you there. Sometimes it kind of freaks me, being out here all alone. Does it ever do that to you?"

"No." I was trailing alongside her, thinking how much I belonged there and how much she belonged on the path.

When we reached the gate, she paused. "You forgot to give me the book."

"Tomorrow. I'll let you have it tomorrow," I said, shamelessly manipulative.

She seemed not to notice. She nodded, then stooped

down to unlock the gate. "Tomorrow," she repeated, then relocked the chain and went to her car.

She waved as she drove away, and when I felt she was well out of earshot, I threw my head back and howled, letting my voice rise above the trees.

I loped through the forest long after the sun had set, trying to burn off my excitement. I repeated the words we had spoken to each other so often that the conversation was indelibly embedded in my brain.

Today, I think, looking out at the forest below me, she'll come again and we'll talk.

I glance over at the tulip bulbs I planted earlier that morning and wonder if I have rooted them properly. It gives me a strange thrill to realize that if I haven't Katherine will show me the correct way to do it. It's a concept that I can't quite accept without making myself crazy. The thought of sharing something with another person, even something as mundane as tulip bulbs, sends me into a cascade of excited yelps.

I hear her car at the foot of the hill and race off into the woods to greet her, thinking of the things we can talk about. About Alovar, about the sweetness of Mandarin oranges, and about ourselves, the selves that we can share. And even though there are many splintered and recondite facets of my own self, there are still enough of them to share with someone. At least this is what I think, or maybe it's what I choose to think.

I WALKED CLEAR out to the kitchen and back without my crutches today. First time I could do that. I used them for the rest of the day, not wanting to put too much pressure on my knee, afraid that if I didn't go slow I'd never be able to get around without them.

Kat came by early this morning for the grocery list and the wagon. I tried to talk to her some, but she said she was in a hurry and wanted to get up to the cabin and back before the sun went down. I let her go, then stood by the window, watching her put the wagon in the back of her little yellow Volkswagen. Watching her pull out of the drive, I kept thinking how lonely she looked. It made me wonder if I looked that same way when I had put that wagon into my car.

Yesterday she hadn't come back until almost dark. Longer than it takes me. Usually when I went up I'd be back by early afternoon. Kat didn't get back to the house until almost five thirty. Waiting for her, I kept telling myself that she didn't know the trail and maybe she was just taking her time, but I knew it was more than that. How much more I could only wait to find out.

When I think of the two of them up there, it scares me. I'm not quite sure why. I know Eddie's too shy to ever actually come out, but he'd talk to her. I know that much. That boy likes to talk. And suddenly having somebody new to talk to would be just too much for him to ignore. I don't know if she's the right person for him to be doing that with. There's probably people out there who could converse with him and understand, but I don't think Kat's one of them. She's too young, too sure of herself. Eddie gets right into talking, and sometimes, without knowing it, he says things that are downright cruel. It's okay with me because I know him, know he hasn't had any practice talking. But someone who doesn't know that—I don't know how'd they take it.

It was hard waiting for her. I kept going to the window, expecting to see her coming down the road. I was up and down so many times I got blisters under both arms from the crutches. The later it got, the more I worried.

What'd happen if she didn't come back? I'd have to tell Jake, and then he'd tell other people, and they'd all go up and search around there. No matter that there was a fence and signs all over the place, they'd walk through that. Only be a matter of time before they found Eddie's cabin. Once they found it, there'd be no way they'd leave him alone. They'd just keep at him until he'd have to come out and show himself. If they ever did see him, no one'd believe anything but the worst. Look at Ted, look at what he believed, and Eddie was his own son.

Around five-thirty I'd heard someone knocking at the back door. I didn't have any idea who it'd be. Everyone I know comes round to the front. Crutching back there, I stood a little ways away from it and called out, "Who's out there?"

"It's me, Annie. Kat."

"My God, girl, what'd you doing coming around back?" I asked, opening that door quicker than I done anything else that day.

"I thought since this was supposed to be a big secret, I'd be better off coming around the back," Kat said, smiling at me, like everything was just fine.

Even with all my worrying about Eddie, I found myself thinking how smart that was. I'd never even given that a thought.

"I mean, think about it, Annie," she said. "Every few weeks you go to the store, stock up on tons of groceries, drive out of town with them, and come back empty. Don't you think people are starting to wonder?"

Kat strode right into the kitchen and to the sink like it was her own.

"I always cover them up real good with a blanket," I said, feeling a little defensive about it.

"Still," Kat shrugged, turning with a glass of water in her hand, "people must wonder. This is a small town," she said, as if she was telling me something I didn't already know.

"They just think I'm odd."

"You are," Kat said, without the faintest hint of a smile.

Seeing that look of hers, I wondered what Eddie had told her.

"You been talking to him, haven't you?"

Kat didn't answer right away. She turned, put her glass in the sink, then walked through the hallway into the living room.

By the time I got there, she was already sitting on the couch, looking through my magazines.

"What'd you talk about?" I asked, standing over her.

"Annie, why don't you sit down and rest."

"What'd you talk to him about?" I asked again, not moving, and letting her know I wasn't going to budge until she told me.

"Come on," Kat said, standing up and leading me over to the couch. "It's okay. We just talked."

"What about?"

"I don't know," she shrugged. "Everything. He's really smart," she said, then quickly went on. "He's never even gone to school. Is that true?"

I nodded, smiling a little bit, unable to keep the pride inside.

"It's hard to believe. He knows so much."

"I started teaching him when he was a baby. He was reading when he was only four years old. Seemed like as soon as he learned that, he couldn't get enough of it. I was going to the library most every day. Got so everybody thought it was me reading all those books."

"You never told them different?"

"No," I answered, before I knew what I was saying, then glanced over at her quickly to see her smile.

"He wasn't burned, was he?"

"'Course he was," I said, looking away, putting my crutches to the side of the couch, trying to remember what I had told her.

"If he was burned, then how come no one knew about him?"

"People knew about him, they just kind of forgot."

"How could they forget you had a son, Annie? It was a small town you were living in at the time. People in small towns don't forget stuff like that."

"They just forgot," I said again, saying it in such a way as to let her know I wasn't going to talk anymore about it.

She looked at me a moment, then leaned back and began paging through her magazine.

"Did he ask about me?"

"Yeah. He said he hoped you were feeling better."

"He said that?"

"Yeah. He did. He sounded worried," Kat said.

I felt tears well up.

"What is it, Annie?"

"Nothing," I said, trying to wave her away and wipe my eyes at the same time.

"You must know he worries about you. You were all he asked about at first."

Still not looking at her, I nodded, thinking about him living up there, about what it must be like to be that alone and know you were always going to be.

"He told me to tell you to take your time and not push yourself. He said it was all right with him that I brought the stuff there," Kat said.

"What'd you mean, it's all right with him?"

"He just said it was okay, didn't bother him any."

"Well, it doesn't matter anyway. My leg's a lot better today, and you've brought enough supplies up there to last him a week or two. By then I should be able to make the trip myself," I said, and waited.

Kat looked nonchalant. "He wants me to come up again," she said.

"Well, I want to thank you for that, but there's no need now that my leg's going to be all right."

"No, he wants me to come up, just to talk."

"Kat . . ."

"It's okay, Annie. He's lonely. He just wants someone to talk to, that's all."

"Kat," I started, trying to find some way to say it, some way to put it that wouldn't sound wrong, "it's not good your going up there. People will find out."

"So what if they find out," she said, suddenly turning on me. "What difference does it make? It's not his fault that he was in an accident. People understand those things. Sure, there's going to be some who are going to make fun of him. But hell, there's always people like that, Annie. They make fun of *me*. Big deal. They're just idiots."

"Kat, it's not like that. It's different, he's . . ." I stopped, not sure what I wanted to say.

"He was burned, right? That's what you told me?"

I nodded. "Yes."

"Well then, if he was burned, people will understand that," she said, examining me closely.

"You don't know what you're doing," I said.

"Then tell me what I'm doing. Tell me the truth, for Christ's sake. You got me going up the mountain to drop off food to some guy who lives in a cabin and won't even come out to say hello. What's wrong with him? How bad could it be?"

"Very bad."

"What do you mean?" she asked softly. "Tell me, please. Annie, trust me."

And for a moment it almost came out, all of it.

"I can't," I finally said, shaking my head. "It's up to Eddie. If he wants you to know, he'll tell you."

"Then I can go up there by myself?" she asked, and I suddenly realized that she wouldn't go if I told her not to. Rather than making me feel any better, this only made me feel worse. I didn't want to be the one to decide. It was too much. What was right or wrong here? Was there a right or wrong?

"Can I go?"

"If Eddie wants you to go up there, it's fine with me," I said, and was surprised when she suddenly put her arms around my shoulders and hugged me. It bothered me that she did that. It bothered me that it meant that much to her.

She told me she was going again tomorrow. I don't know what'll come of this. Does Eddie know what he's doing? I wish I could talk to him, but I still have another week or so before I'll be able to make the trip. It seems like an awfully long time.

What if she suddenly stops going? What will that do to Eddie? Would he understand that she's just a girl, barely old enough to know what she wants?

But then, Eddie himself is only a few years older than she. Why do I always think of him as being so old? Maybe because he's had to be, and I guess because it scares me to think of him being young. The young make such stupid mistakes, and it's only their being young that makes it all right. They have all the time in the world to make up for them. But Eddie, how much time does Eddie have?

"What do you think?" I grunt impatiently, peering out at her from behind my curtain.

She sprawls across the front step of my porch and holds up a hand to quiet me.

I growl beneath my breath.

"You sure make a lot of noises," she says.

I bare my teeth and hunker down by the window. I light another cigarette and examine her. Today she's wearing a white shirt with red embroidery on the front. Her pants are baggy green ones with black stitching across the right knee. Around her shoulders is draped a light brown sweater. Her hair fascinates me. Staring at her bowed head, I can see the clean line of her scalp beneath the purple and orange strands. The wind ruffles it, parting the silky hairs. Looking at her, I wonder what it would be like to touch her. Thinking this, I find my hand drifting. I consciously pull it away from the windowsill.

I find myself looking first at my hand and then hers, comparing the two. The long graceful line of her fingers enthralls me, and when I look at the short stubby digits that sprout out of my own knuckles, it's hard to even believe that both of these objects are the same.

Katherine marks her place with a finger and closes the book.

"What do you think?" I ask again.

"It's okay," she answers hesitantly.

"What do you mean, okay?"

"It's all right."

"What's wrong with it?" I ask immediately, sensing her unease.

"Well, I don't know. Alovar," she says, then pauses. "He . . ."

"Yes, what about him?"

"He's just so alone. I mean, he doesn't have anything. All he's got is his sword."

"But that's the point of it, all he needs is his sword. That's what makes him what he is. It's what defines him."

"I don't see it that way."

"How do you see it?"

"I see him as someone who doesn't know what he wants, and because all he has is this weapon, that's all he ever becomes."

"That's ridiculous," I growl, finding her criticism unpleasant. I've never been criticized before. John always loves my things.

"No, it isn't ridiculous, Edward. All Alovar seems to do is run around flexing his muscles and killing people."

"That's not it at all. He's the reawakening consciousness of his people. He personifies what they can be and what they once were."

"I don't think that comes across," Katherine says, shaking her head. "He just seems like another Mad Max to me."

"Who's Mad Max?"

"You don't *know* who Mad Max is?"

She sounds so incredulous that I feel guilty about my ignorance.

"Mad Max, the Road Warrior. You've *never* heard of him?"

"No."

"Jesus, Edward, you ought to get a VCR or something up here."

"No electricity."

"So get a generator."

"No way to get it up here. The old woman would never be able to manage it."

"Why do you call her the old woman?"

"It's what she is."

"No, she isn't. She's your mother."

"Mothers are old ladies, it's axiomatic."

"Not necessarily. There's people who have children when they're only in their teens."

"Yes, but they'll always be considered old by their children."

She sighs in exasperation, "You know, sometimes talking to you isn't a lot of fun."

"Why?"

She ignores this. "Is Alovar supposed to be you?"

"Of course not."

"I thought all writers write about themselves."

"I don't know about all writers. I only know about me, and Alovar is certainly not me."

"Not even a little?"

"Maybe a small part of him."

She smiles knowingly, "How about a large part of him? He's in exile too, same as you."

"I'm not in exile. I prefer the woods," I say a bit pompously.

Katherine doesn't even comment on this. "What's your very first book like?"

"*The Abomination?*"

"Yeah. That's the only one that isn't about Alovar, right?"

"Yes, that was my first."

"What's it about?"

"It's about a person born in the next century," I say.

"Yeah?" she prompts.

"Yes."

"You don't want to tell me about it."

"I'd rather not."

"You know I can just get it from the bookstore."

"I know that."

"So why won't you tell me about it?"

"Look at that," I say, "over by that clearing, that cloud there. What does that one look like?"

Sometimes this works. I have discovered that Katherine is a confirmed cloud reader. She loves to examine each passing one until she discovers its cryptic shape.

She cranes her neck. It is infinitely graceful.

"Richard Nixon," she says. "See the nose."

I examine the cloud formation carefully, looking for the nose without much success.

"Whatever happened to your father?" she asks, turning back to my window.

"He died," I say curtly.

"Long ago?"

"Quite a while."

"It must have been hard for you and your mother then."

And for a moment I almost tell her what it was really like, how much easier it suddenly was without him. If I had known it would be like that, I would have forced things to happen long before they did.

"It wasn't that difficult. That was when we moved here."

"How was that?"

"What?"

"Moving. How did you do it?"

I remember the van and the way the world suddenly seemed to open up to me. Traveling across the country, storing up every bit of visual memory I could, knowing that it might never be possible again.

"We bought a van with tinted windows."

"Did you ever go outside while you were traveling?"

"At night, if there was no one around, sometimes she would let me out for a while," I say softly, leaning against the window frame, smoking, remembering the taste of that night air so long ago. The scents that drifted to me, scents I had only read about but never dreamed I would ever actually know.

When I glance over at Katherine, she's crying.

"What? What is it?"

She waves her hand at me and turns away.

"Come on, tell me." I say, feeling my teeth gnashing my upper lip.

"Look at that one," Katherine suddenly says, pointing off to the south.

I twist around to see a huge bilious cloud drifting across the sky.

"It looks like freedom," she says, and when I turn to look at her, I see she has averted her face.

"He was my first," she tells me, and I know I don't want to hear this, but at the same time can't help myself from wanting to know everything about it. "I didn't really like him that much. It was more like it was something I just had to get done. You know what I mean?" She is looking at my window.

I nod.

She seems to sense this and goes on.

"We did it in his car," she snorts. "Can you imagine that. That's every cliché in the world. It wasn't even a very nice car." She pauses for a moment, thoughtful. "It was a green car with a black interior, and we climbed into the backseat and he stuck it in me. That's all there was to it. I didn't even know what we were doing before it was over. And then, listen to this, Edward, you'll love this. Then he kind of rolls off of me, lights a cigarette, and asks, 'How was it for you?' I couldn't help it. I just started laughing and couldn't stop. I was still laughing when he dropped me off in front of my house. It would've been okay but both of my parents were home, and I remember I walked into the house and they kept asking me what was wrong: 'Kat, what's wrong?' And when I tried to tell them that everything was all right, I found I wasn't laughing anymore. I was crying." She stops, shakes her head, smiles.

A moment later she turns and asks, "Don't you think that's hysterical?"

"No," I whisper.

"Neither do I," she says softly, and turns away.

We watch the sun drift into the west. Katherine points out yet more clouds and tells me what they are. I nod, grunt, and agree with her, so taken with her that I'm thinking about dyeing my own hair orange and purple. I wonder how much dye it would take.

"You know about my Uncle Jake?" she asks.

"My Uncle Jake?"

"No," she smiles. "*My* Uncle Jake. He's just Jake to you, unless you know something I don't."

"Who is he?"

"So you don't then, huh?"

"Who is he?" I repeat.

"He's kind of seeing your mother."

"Oh."

"That's it?" she says, looking at my window curiously. "That's all you have to say about it?"

"Yes."

"You don't want to *know* anything about him, or them?"

"Not really, no."

"Why?"

I shrug.

"He's a nice guy," she says. "He's my favorite relative. When they gave me a choice of him or Aunt Edna in New York, I picked him, even though I'd rather be in New York."

"I'm glad you picked him."

"So am I," she says, glancing quickly in my direction.

I blush, feeling every hair on my body stand on end.

"I have to go now," she says, pushing herself to her feet and brushing off the backs of her legs.

I watch her move, admiring her grace and suppleness.

"You going to walk with me?" she says.

"I'll catch up."

She starts up the hill and I unbolt the door and open it. I dart across the porch and into the woods. Just as I enter the woods, I see her turn to look back. Her glance freezes everything inside my chest.

I race quickly through the trees to the other side of the hill and anxiously wait for her, dreading what she might have seen.

I wait a long time before she finally appears.

"Are you there?" she says, peering into the underbrush.

"Yes."

"Was that you?"

A moment passes. "Yes," I answer.

She nods and begins to walk down the hill. I follow, wanting to ask what she's seen and what she thought of what she saw. I can't form the words.

We walk silently to the gate.

She unlocks it, steps to the other side, then leans her chin on one of the crossbars.

"I didn't see you," she calls, then bends over and latches and locks the chain. "But if I had, it wouldn't have mattered, Edward," she says and waits for my response.

"Good-bye, Katherine," I call from beneath the pines, and watch her turn and slide into her car.

I stand long after she's gone, wondering about her. It's hard for me to think of anything else anymore. I haven't written in days and can't seem to think of a word to write, other than the obvious one. And this one is so utterly impossible, I try not to even think it.

The sun fades, leaving me alone in the shadows. I wait until it's completely dark before I step out onto the path and walk toward home. The darkness moves around me like a friend. For the first time in my life, I find its companionship intolerable.

CHAPTER
12

I SAW MY son today. First time in over three weeks. I managed to get up there without bothering my knee too much. Doc Calken wanted me to take it easy for a few more days, but I figured I felt well enough to make the trip, and I was worried about what was going on up there.

For the last two weeks I've stood by my window and watched that little yellow bug of Kat's drive by, knowing exactly where she was headed. It was starting to scare me about what could be happening up there. Now, after having seen Eddie, I don't know if I feel any less frightened.

It surprised me some the way things turned out. I went up to the cabin, just the way I always do, and knew he knew I was there. I stepped up to the porch and called out to him, expecting him to act the way he's been acting for almost the last year now. It surprised me what he did. He came right out onto the porch, first time I called. I was so startled by him I didn't even know what to say.

"How are you feeling?" was the first thing he said to me.

Looking at him standing there, watching me, I didn't know what I was feeling.

"Why don't you come inside and rest," he said, stepping down from the porch and taking my arm.

I was still so shocked by the whole thing I just let him lead me.

Inside, the cabin was different. At first I couldn't figure out what it was, then I noticed that curtains hung from all the windows. For the life of me, I couldn't figure out why he'd need curtains up there, him being so alone and all. Later when I thought about it, I couldn't believe I didn't see the reason right off.

Then I saw the chair. At first I thought it was the one I'd seen such a long time ago, broken and thrown out with the trash. I just stared at it, then looked at Eddie. He wouldn't meet my eye.

"Why don't you sit and rest," he said, leading me over to the chair, "and I'll make us some coffee."

I sat down, running my hands over the arms of it, realizing that it wasn't a bit like that other one at all. It was sturdier and didn't creak and shift beneath me.

He was standing by the cook stove, pouring out the coffee. I could tell he knew I was watching him by the hairs on the back of his neck. He never could quite control them. They were always standing on end, regardless of how much he tried to pretend they weren't. Sitting back, feeling the chair beneath me, realizing what it meant, made me feel almost like crying. It was like having a son again.

It has always seemed to me a hard thing for a child to forgive his parents for something, and even harder for parents to realize that they need their child's forgiveness. My son had forgiven me for what I had done.

"Your leg all right?" Eddie asked, handing me my coffee.

"A little sore, but not too bad," I allowed, looking around the cabin, noticing the curtains.

"I made them," Eddie said, unable to keep the pride out of his voice.

I looked over at him and he glanced away sheepishly. "I used some old blankets I had and stitched them together."

"They're nice," I nodded. "You done a good job," I said and took another sip of my coffee and ran my hand along the smooth arm of the chair.

Eddie tilted his head shyly. "I thought you might need to sit."

"Much nicer than that other one. You learned some since then."

"Yes."

We sat for a while without saying anything, just being comfortable with each other. I tried to remember the last time we'd been able to do that and I couldn't.

"You been doing okay then, I guess?"

"Yes."

"Food held out all right while I was laid up?"

"A few bad days. Nothing extreme."

"Must have worried you some, me not showing up."

"No," Eddie said, and met my glance. "I knew you'd come."

Eddie rose to refill our cups. As he was pouring my coffee he asked, "How's Jake?"

The question startled me enough so that my hand fluttered and caused him to spill. Eddie set aside the pot and stooped down to wipe up the mess.

"It's okay," Eddie said, still crouched before me. And before I could help it I put my hand on his shoulder. He didn't pull away.

"It's okay," he said again softly, then rose and went to the stove.

"She told you about him?" I said.

"Yes."

"It's not anything, Eddie. He's just a friend, just someone I spend some time with. I don't want you—"

Eddie turned and raised his hand, stopping me. "It's all right. You don't have to explain this to me. I shouldn't have ever made you feel as if you had to explain."

It's hard for me to admit this, but there's been times when I hated Eddie, when I actually hated my own son.

Wasn't anything he could help, didn't have anything to do with who he is or what he looks like. It was because I knew he was up there, waiting for me.

I didn't want to be a mother anymore. I wanted to be a woman again. I know at my age that doesn't make a lot of sense, but making sense isn't something humans seem to care too much about. It was my suddenly being on my own, and realizing Eddie didn't want me with him anymore—that's what I think did it. And of course all those years with Ted, bad years towards the end, that made me realize, all of a sudden, how much I missed being alive. I had been dead, as cut off as Eddie was up there in the attic.

Took me a while to get started. Once I got the hang of it, I just went crazy. All that running around and carrying on seems kind of foolish to me now, but at the time I was doing it no one could tell me different.

I remember once, lying up with Jim Harbinger, and him telling me how after his wife died he decided he was just going to have a good time. He was tired of being "things"—a husband, a provider, all that other stuff. He just wanted to be himself, and there wasn't no one that could tell him anymore to be something else. I guess that's what I felt. I'd been a mother and a wife for just about my whole life. That I didn't have to be either anymore, made me run crazy. It made me forget that things don't work that way. People don't conveniently step in and out of your world just because you get tired of having to care for them. There's some people that are just yours for your whole life, no matter what. And I guess, in all honesty, I wouldn't want it any different.

Eddie's never been the easiest boy in the world, but trying to imagine my life without him makes it seem like the loneliest existence I could ever think of.

I was pondering all this while I was watching him by the cook stove, sitting in the chair he had made, knowing what must have been in his mind when he made it.

"She tell you to make this?" I said.

Eddie turned, baring his teeth at me sheepishly. "No, not the chair. But we talked about you."

"And what did she say?"

Eddie stepped to the window. He pulled back the curtain. The sky was blue.

"She said you were my mother."

I fussed with my cup. "That surprise you, did it?"

"No." Eddie turned to me. "I'd always noticed the family resemblance," he said and we both laughed.

So I owe her that much. She gave me back my boy. I didn't much like the way she was going up there every day, but it seemed, at that moment, that maybe it was all right. Maybe she was helping him some to live his life.

Jake came by this evening, asking me about Kat. Said he never saw her anymore and wanted to know if I knew where she was going all the time. I told him that I hadn't talked to her for a while, which was a lie. But what else could I say to him? I can't say where she goes. If I tell him that, then I have to tell him everything, and I don't know if he should know all of it.

People who know about him don't have much in the way of good luck. None of it's Eddie's fault, but it doesn't change what happened.

Like old Doc Andestad dying on the way home after delivering Eddie. He drove his '68 Chevy Malibu right off the road at Jericho Bend. At the time I hadn't thought much about it. I was too concerned with other things. Later, after all that happened with Ted, I realized how it was something I should have always known. Ted had killed him.

He told me he hadn't set out to do that. It just kind of happened. And after it had, Ted went on about how it seemed more an act of God than anything else. It would keep our secret safe, he'd said, looking at me, wanting me to believe him. I didn't then and still don't.

Seemed Ted and the Doc sat up in the kitchen, drinking and talking about what they should do about Eddie. Doc said he thought it was some kind of medical miracle and should be studied. Ted didn't want anything like that happening to our son, or so he claimed. But I know now all he really cared about was people finding out that he was the father. He couldn't've lived with that.

It was easy for him to keep plying Doc with drinks and then offering to drive him back. Easy as pie, as Ted used to say. Doc never made it home. Ted told me he felt bad about it, but he also felt like he was protecting his son from all those people. That's just how he put it. I think that was the only time I ever heard Ted refer that way to Eddie—his son. And even then it didn't come out too easy for him. Seemed more like he spit it out than said it.

"She comes up here most every day now, doesn't she?" I

asked, leaning back in my chair, admiring the way it held and didn't give.

"Yes."

"You talk to her much?"

"Yes."

"That's why the curtains, isn't it?"

"Yes. I can look out, she can't look in."

"She wants to, though, doesn't she?"

"Yes, she does."

I took a sip of my coffee, Eddie lit another cigarette. "You going to let her?"

"Look inside?"

"Yeah, look inside."

"I don't know," Eddie answered, peering at me closely, trying to find an answer.

"You never done that before," I said.

Eddie snorted. "I've never known anyone before. Just you and him."

"We love you."

Eddie only looked at me.

"I love you, I mean."

Eddie went over to the fireplace. I noticed he'd combed his hair.

"She keeps asking."

"You tell her, no?"

"I tell her, maybe."

Just thinking about that conversation makes me shake my head. The boy's in love with her. I keep wondering what that must feel like to him. He's never been with anyone, never talked to anyone before. I should have known it would happen. How couldn't it happen? I guess I kept thinking that they would be friends, and that maybe it'd be okay for Eddie to have a friend. All he's ever had is me, and for a long time that was enough. But now I wonder if it'll ever be enough, after this.

What's going to happen to him when she leaves, and she will. She's not going to stay here. What will that do to Eddie? If you're always lonely you never really know what you're missing. But once something's lost, it's always not going to be there. How's he going to go on after this ends?

"You think you will?" I said.

"I don't know. I don't know how I can." Eddie shrugged. His lip was bleeding. "Look at me," he said, holding his arms out. "How could I show her this and expect her to see anything else."

I looked at him, my son. It had been a long time since I had. The bunched-up shoulders. The dangling, twisted arms covered with hair.

I shook my head, not knowing what to say.

He let his arms drop to his sides and turned back to the fireplace.

I went to him and put my arm on his shoulder. All I could feel was the warmth of him beneath the smoothly combed mat of hair.

Kat came by. Said she'd been real busy and just couldn't find the time to stop in. We both knew that wasn't true, but neither of us said anything.

She asked me if Jake had been talking about her. I told her he had, and that he had been wondering where she was going all the time.

She said, "He keeps asking me the same thing."

"What do you tell him?" I asked, thinking how many

secrets each of us suddenly had, and wondering if I could trust her with mine.

"I tell Uncle Jake I'm exploring."

"What's he say to that?"

"He says I should be careful. But then I catch him looking at me like he doesn't believe me." She reached down and reshuffled the magazines on my table.

"I went to see Eddie yesterday," I said, and looked at her closely.

"How is he?" she smiled.

"He's fine," I said, more curtly than I had planned, not liking the way she smiled. "He made a chair," I said, trying to make up for the way I'd just sounded.

"He told me." Kat was nearly beaming.

"He did a good job," I said.

"Better than the last one?"

"He told you about that?"

"Yes, he did," she said, letting me know how far things had gone.

"He's told me a lot of things."

What am I supposed to do? I wish somebody would tell me what to do because I don't know. All I know is, the two of them are going to hurt each other. There's no other way for this to end, and I could see she was as confused as he was.

"How come he won't come out to me?" she asked. "He comes out for you."

"That's something that he has to decide."

"Well, just tell me, how bad is he hurt?"

"Bad enough."

"That's not any kind of an answer, Annie. Why can't you just trust me with this. You've trusted me with everything else."

"And look at where that's gotten us," I said, without thinking.

"*Where?*" Kat demanded, standing up. "Where has that gotten you? I'll tell you where it's gotten you. It's gotten you inside and into a chair he built for you. Don't you understand him at all? He's up there all alone, for Christ's sake. He's been alone for almost eight years. Don't you know what that does to somebody, especially somebody as sensitive as he is. It must make him half crazy. How you can sit there and talk to me about what *I've* done to him?"

"Don't you lecture me. Don't you ever. You don't have any idea what you're talking about," I paused, trembling. "You come waltzing in here, thinking you know everything. Well, let me tell you something, Katherine Mancy, you don't know one thing about that boy up there and what's going on with him. I've been taking care of him for longer than you've been alive, so don't you try to tell me what's good or bad about what I've done," I finished, glaring at her, daring her to say one more word to me.

She turned away and stepped to the bureau. She picked up a picture and held it. It was a picture of me and Ted before Eddie was born.

"Tell me about him?" she asked, and for a moment the way she said "him" reminded me so much of Eddie, I couldn't speak. "Tell me about your husband, Annie," she said, holding the picture out, as if our whole conversation a moment before hadn't taken place.

"Kat," I said, shaking my head. "Put it down. There's nothing to say about him."

"Eddie won't even talk about him. He just says that he died. That's all."

"Kat, there's things that you're better off not knowing.

There's things that are more painful than any of us care to admit. Bringing them back up will only start the pain all over again."

"Don't you think talking about them might make the pain go away?"

"No, it's not like that."

"How do you know unless you try?"

"I know," I said, and waited until she put the picture back down before I patted the couch beside me and told her to set herself down. We talked some.

She knew so much about us, it scared me. Not so much what she knew but what she didn't know. It seems like those missing pieces are the pieces that can destroy everything we've managed to build here. I know she doesn't want that to happen, but that doesn't mean it won't. Wanting something, I had learned, didn't have a whole lot to do with what happened. Sometimes it seemed to me that that was all a person was made for: to want. Isn't one thing it's another, and none of those things ever seemed to work out anywhere near the way you planned.

Yesterday, at Eddie's, he asked me what Kat looked like when I saw her in town. I didn't know what he meant until he asked me what she wore when I saw her. After I described what I remembered about her clothes, he smiled and asked me what she looked like when she was walking down the sidewalk. I couldn't understand what he was talking about and told him so.

"What does she look like when she's coming up the drive to your house? Do you see her face or her hair first, or do you notice her clothes? And when she comes inside, does she sit down or does she wait for you to sit?" He looked at me eagerly.

I couldn't answer. I couldn't accept the hunger I saw. He

wanted to know, I suppose, if she was the same person in town that she was up there, with him.

"He tell you," Kat suddenly asked, "about the mandarin oranges?"

"Yes," I nodded. "And the tulips, and the snails and all."

"I try to bring him something different every time I go. He tell you what he did with the snails?"

"No."

Kat suddenly threw her head back and laughed, "He ate the whole shell. I could hear him in there crunching it. I thought he was going to choke to death."

I grinned, thinking about that, thinking how it'd be just like Eddie to stuff the whole thing in his mouth and chew away, not having the faintest idea what he was doing. "What'd he say about them?"

"He said he thought they were too noisy to eat." Kat laughed, then began telling about the tulips, how she'd had to dig them up and replant them all over again, how Eddie'd put them in upside down.

I liked it. I liked being able to talk to somebody about him. Ted never listened to anything I'd say about him. He'd just grunt, then walk away. I'd never sat with anyone before and talked like this. It was nice, but even so, there was still that worry that wouldn't go away.

When I'd left the cabin, Eddie had walked me down to the gate. He'd never done that before. He told me he always walked Katherine back, of course he kept to the woods when he did it. But with me, he walked right along beside me.

"I read one of his books." Kat said.

"Did you. Did you like it?" It was something that I had never been able to share with him and had trouble understanding.

"It was okay," she shrugged, "but I thought it was going to be better than what it was."

"Which one did you read?"

"*Alovar.* I guess it's the first one in the series."

"He tell you about his first book?"

"*The Abomination?*"

"Yeah."

"Just that it was different," she paused to look at me. "Did you read it? He said you didn't like his books very much."

"True, I never did much care for them. Seems like there's so much killing and fighting going on that it was hard to tell who was doing what to who."

"Did you read his first one?"

"Which one was that again?" I said, sorry I'd ever started on this.

"*The Abomination?*" she said.

"No, I don't think I did finish that one."

"You *never* read the first thing he wrote? His first book?" She had an incredulous look on her face.

"No, can't say that I did."

"What about—" she started, but I interrupted her by standing up and moving off to the kitchen. I poured us some lemonade and carried it back inside.

The Abomination, that was the name of his first book, and the last thing Ted ever said to him. I can still see Ted up in the attic, glaring at Eddie huddled in the corner with the ax lying beside his hand.

"You aren't my son! You're an abomination!" Ted screamed, moving towards him, reaching for the ax, but Eddie was faster. He snatched it up first and moved away from him, towards the stairs, towards me.

In the book, a small deformed child is born to a family

living at some time in the future. Everyone wants to kill it, but the mother hides it and then sneaks off to the end of the world. That's what it's called, this place they go to, The End Of The World.

No one ever bothers them there because everyone's afraid of the place. And the few people who do come there are always frightened off by the sight of the child, who has now grown into maturity. The child is a monster to all but the mother who cares for him and loves him.

While they live there, the family tries to find them. They search everywhere before someone tells them about the monster that lives and protects The End of The World. The family immediately knows who this is and they go there, thinking they'll once and for all end this thing they've started.

When they finally come to this place, they trap the monster who's their brother and their son. They tie him on the ground and the father says, "It is time to rid the world of this abomination against nature and God." But before he can do so, the mother attacks him. In their struggle she manages to free her son but dies in the melee. The son rises with the ax in his hand and slays his family. He stands over his father and, swinging the ax one last time, howls into the sky and brings the blade down into his father's skull, splitting it apart and bringing the end of the world to all the world. *For he who murders his father, murders all.* The last sentence of the book. I still remember it. Can't imagine a time when I won't.

Kat said she was planning on going up to see him tomorrow morning and asked if I wanted to come along.

I wanted to but knew my knee wouldn't take another trek so soon. I told her I'd like that, but I needed to rest a bit before I made the trip again.

I'd like to see the two of them together, see how they act

with each other. It's hard to imagine them talking as much as they do. I know Eddie can talk, he's always had that in him, but trying to picture him talking to Kat seems strange. But then I've never seen him talk to anyone else. Seems like such a strange thing to me, never talking but to one person.

Is this fair to him, what she's doing? I wish I knew. There isn't even anyone I can talk to, only Kat, and she's the problem.

Just doesn't seem fair sometimes that all of this had to happen to us. Why couldn't everybody just leave us alone? Everything's confused now.

This girl's changing everything. She's making me suddenly realize all the things Eddie's missed. Yet I don't think this is good, because they're things he can't ever have. What's it going to be like when he realizes this? When he finally knows that what he has is all he can ever have?

CHAPTER
13

ALOVAR DECIDED HER voice was coming from one of the broken buildings but he made no move to approach. He remained by the dying embers of his campfire.

"Mandarin orange," she said.

"I have never tasted anything like that before," he answered.

"I found it."

"Where?" he said, and listened to the answering silence. He shrugged, then asked, "How long have you been here?"

"Why didn't you kill me when you could?" she said, ignoring his question.

"That is not my way."

"You knew I was watching you."

"There are worse things than being watched." Alovar reached for his tea. He sipped it, inhaling the hot steam, trying to work the morning chill out of his bones.

"I have heard of you. You are called Warrior."

"I am Alovar."

"No. Maybe once, but no longer. Here there are no names." She paused. "You are from the Realm?"

"Once, a long time ago, I was of the Realm."

"Did they cast you out?"

"Yes."

"Are you a mutant?"

"Are you?"

"No."

"Then neither am I."

"Why do you say it like that?"

"Because I am different from everyone else."

"Better?"

"Not to those who count."

"Those who count, count only rocks."

"That may be, but it does not change the world."

"There is no world. There is only us and what we do each moment."

Alovar nodded, finding a logic in the woman's words.

"And you," he said, "are you from the Realm also?"

"I am from everywhere—from nowhere."

"That is what they say about The Warrior."

"Yes, and you are he."

"For a time, until someone stronger comes along." Alovar squinted towards the building, where he heard a noise. She appeared at the corner of it. Her form was so clean and unmarked that he found it difficult to look away.

"I am also different from anyone else. My differences frighten them. They are mindless fools who think the world is what they see each day."

"Isn't it?"

"No, it is what will be tomorrow."

"And today?"

"Today is only preparation," she replied, crouching down on her heels at a safe distance from where he sat.

Alovar nodded, then slowly brought out another cup. He filled it with tea and set it on the other side of his cook fire.

A moment later she stood before him. She warily stooped to pick up the tea.

"I found these," Alovar said, nodding to the piles of books.

"I have seen them before," she said, glancing down at them, then quickly back to Alovar. "The old world must have been beautiful."

"I do not think so."

"Why?"

"Look at these," Alovar said, reaching across for one of the books. She stepped back quickly, watching him closely.

Alovar pretended not to notice as he sifted through the pile and chose one. He threw it across to her and settled back.

She picked it up gingerly, opened it, her eyes darting back and forth, from the pages to Alovar.

"I see only beauty," she said.

"Nothing else?" Alovar asked. Her glance was curious. She went back to the book, looking more closely, trusting him.

She said, "Other things, but none that take away the perfection of the people."

"And these things?" Alovar opened a book and pointed to the objects he had discovered were weapons.

"I do not know what these things are for," she said, "but they are well made."

"They are weapons. Look," Alovar said, and turned the pages, showing her how the objects worked.

"Their mouths *bite*?" she asked, incredulous.

Alovar nodded and turned to another page. On it was a drawing of a man hidden behind a hill, leveling one of the slender tubes at a group of people, so far in the distance, it was difficult to even discern their faces.

"It is not possible," she said, looking at him, trying to find the deception.

"I think it is. I think these people," Alovar said, turning to a drawing of one of the beautiful people, "kill only for the killing. I think they like it and grow more beautiful with it. All of these things, these sky things and land things are for killing. Death made their users beautiful. The more they destroyed, the more beautiful they became." Alovar did not want to believe what he was saying.

The woman looked up. She examined each of his features. She nodded. "You are beautiful, too. As beautiful as they."

Alovar nodded.

"Do you feed on death?" she said.

Alovar shook his head.

"Yet you are The Warrior. They even say your sword cuts through stone."

"Who are those who say this?"

"The ones I have heard here, the ones who pass through and camp but stay only briefly. This place frightens them."

"But not you?"

"No. Not me," she said.

Alovar placed the paper book on top of a pile.

She watched him closely, then squatted down and placed her book in its proper pile. "They each have the same signs on their faces," she said, examining the piles.

"Yes, I think this was their language."

"Can you read these signs?" she asked excitedly.

Alovar shook his head.

She started to rise, then paused, glanced at him warily, and slowly sat on her heels. She sipped her tea, watching him over the rim. And it was in this way that Alovar met his first and only friend.

. . .

She led through the ruined city, showing him things he had overlooked.

"There are rooms beneath the rooms you see," she explained. Seeing his confusion, she smiled and said, "Come, I will show you," and took him into one of the broken buildings, walked confidently across its hard metal floor to a corner, paused there and stooped. She pointed. "What do you see here?"

Alovar examined the floor carefully, but saw no difference in its textures. "Nothing."

"Here," she told him, suddenly reaching down to push against the floor. As soon as she did this, a handle popped up from its surface. The action startled Alovar and, before he could stop himself, he had stepped back and half drawn his sword.

The woman, stood facing him, her hand beneath her robe.

Alovar slowly released his sword and stepped towards this new discovery. He ignored her movement, giving her the moment to use as she would.

"See," she said, withdrawing her hand from her robe and, stooping again, pointed to the floor. "These old ones built passages in their floors to hide in."

She showed him how the secret doors could be discovered by finding the slightly wider creases built into the face of the floor.

She popped the door opened and stepped down. Alovar was reluctant to follow into this dark passage.

"Come, it's safe. I have been down here many times before," she said, and disappeared from sight.

Alovar followed, his hand on his scabbard.

Beneath the floor he found a large stone room, empty of everything but a few scattered pieces of wood.

"Are all of these rooms like this?" Alovar asked, trying to discern what possible use it could have had.

"Some are different," she shrugged, and Alovar could tell by her answer that there was more than she was willing to explain.

"I think this is where they hid when they were being attacked," she said, patting the stone wall. "Nothing would get through these."

"Something did," Alovar said.

What would the ancient people have done about food and drink if they were forced to hide? Wondering this, he remembered the taste of her gift.

She led him further into the ruined city, pointing out the buildings she had explored and those that she had found too broken to chance entering. In one of the unbroken structures, she preceded him into a stairway. It seemed to climb forever. Alovar followed cautiously, occasionally stopping to test the steps beneath his feet, and each time she glanced back and smiled.

At the top they reached a doorway that would surely lead only into emptiness. She reached for it and pushed forward. Alovar tried to stop her. She easily twisted out of his grip and turned with her hand beneath her tunic.

"Do not touch me," she said quietly. "Do not touch me again." She turned back to the door. "This is safe. I would not lead you into a trap." She pushed through.

Alovar sighed and followed.

For a moment he felt as if he had stepped right out into the sky, for it surrounded him and held him up. He caught his breath, unable to believe.

The horizon rose up from all around him and stretched far beyond his sight. The buildings and the ancient city lay far below and seemed small and insignificant. He caught her looking at him, smiling. She nodded, then turned and pointed.

Alovar followed the direction of her arm. Off in the distance he could see a darker patch hovering over the burnt lands.

"That is the beginning of the Realm."

Alovar stared at this dark shadow so far away, finding it difficult to accept that it could be the Realm. He knew it would take a full seven days of travel to reach, but from this great height it seemed undeniably close.

Cautiously he crossed the roof to the very edge and peered down. The wall fell straight downward to the city far below. The city seemed even further away than the Realm. He glanced back and forth between these two images, trying to understand this difference.

"I do not understand this either," she said, stepping up beside him to look down. "Things that are close look far, while things that are far look much closer," she shrugged. "It makes no sense."

Alovar nodded, unable to speak, finding the sky a welcome respite from the life below.

"There," Alovar said, pointing into the sky at a huge bilious cloud floating across its face. "What would it feel like to touch them?"

"Maybe the ancient ones knew," she said.

"Their knowledge did them little good," Alovar replied. Silently she turned back to the stairwell. Alovar followed as they started their descent.

"Katherine," she said.

Alovar nodded. Softly he repeated the name to himself. He stared at her across the fire and watched the way the flames flickered shadows across her face. He examined her closely, attempting again to find some sign of imperfection.

She became aware of his glaze and met it. Then they turned away from each other in embarrassment.

"You have been here a long time?" Alovar asked.

"Yes," she answered curtly, and volunteered nothing more.

"Alone?"

"Sometimes."

Alovar waited for her to go on. When she didn't, he fed the fire.

"And you, have you always been alone?" she said.

"Yes, always."

"Even in the Realm."

"There, too. I was part of the Circle."

She nodded, watching the fire grow.

"These people who pass through here, are there many and who are they?"

"Some are Marauders, some are bands of mutants looking for safety."

"They never stay?"

"No, they are always frightened by the city. You are the first who has stayed." She paused, looking at him. "It doesn't frighten you?"

"No," Alovar replied. "It is dead. The dead no longer frighten me. Only the living."

"They frighten me as well. Each time they come I worry that one of them will stay."

"Even the mutants?"

"The mutants would only bring the Marauders, and if the Marauders ever lose their fear, then I will lose the city." She stared into the fire. "It is all I know now. It would be difficult.

Alovar shifted his weight.

"Will you stay?" she asked, without inflection, giving him little indication how she wanted him to answer.

"For a while, if it does not trouble you."

She nodded and rose to her feet. She stood for a moment, then turned and disappeared into the shadows beyond the fire.

Alovar cocked his head, trying to hear her, but heard only the wind whistling through the city.

He sat watching his fire, thinking of the secrets the place still kept, wondering if there might be more that even Katherine had not discovered. Thinking this, he found her name readily on his lips. It surprised him—the ease with which it seemed to rest there.

For three days they traversed the city together. Each day Katherine took him to new sections and showed him her discoveries. Alovar was amazed by what he saw. These people had invented every possible object required for comfort. Their lives must have been filled with great luxury, which would explain their easy beauty.

He and Katherine would discuss this, trying to decide why, with all that these people had, why they would seek their pleasures in war.

Alovar had showed her all of his paper books and the drawings inside them. Together they had examined the faces that seemed to relish destruction, and marveled at the ease with which this was accomplished by their strange inventions. They both pondered this, finding it impossible to understand that if there was so much for everyone, how could they still fight?

In the paper books there were drawings of huge fields of corn, crops beyond anything either of them had ever seen or heard told of. These people did not war for food. What reasons did this leave? What else was there that would necessitate this constant search for destruction? Neither of them could fathom it. The more they spoke, the more important the answer became to them.

Each evening Katherine now shared his fire. They would talk. As the night grew later, she would ask if he would leave the next day, never displaying any indication that it mattered to her.

After Alovar answered, she would disappear silently into the night. He thought about attempting to follow her, to see where she went, but he refrained, allowing her the privacy she desired.

She brought him strange foods to taste, things she had found in the city. She would appear in the morning by his campsite bearing these gifts, then watch as he ate, anxious to hear his thoughts. Once she brought something that mystified him. He opened the can eagerly, having come to know how wonderful these things could be. After staring into the opened can, he looked at her in confusion. She nodded her encouragement. Alovar pulled out an ineatable looking morsel. She nodded again, and Alovar popped it into his mouth, chewing strenuously to mulch the food. He stopped when he heard her laughter.

"No," she told him. "Not like that, like this," she said, reaching across to pull one from the can. She took it, and drawing out her knife, speared it into the mouth of the thing. The point came out, bearing a soft, wet-looking creature, which she took into her own mouth and chewed with obvious enjoyment.

Alovar spit out bits of something that tasted like stone and followed her directions. He found her method much better, and quickly finished off the rest of the can's contents. For the remainder of the day she teased him about this, pointing out small bits of wood and stone, saying he might like to try them as well.

He found himself missing her during the times she disappeared. This surprised him, for he had never felt this sensation before. He had taken women in the Realm but they had been only for pleasure. He had never sought them out for their company, and he realized suddenly that he had never sought out *anyone* for companionship, male or female. It surprised him, for it was something he had never thought about before and found vaguely disquieting to think about now.

Katherine told him little of her life in the city before his appearance. He would ask her, phrasing his questions differently each time, but she always avoided them. This made him all the more curious, yet he tried to restrain himself, sensing that she would answer these things when she felt it appropriate.

They began to carry the paper books with them when they explored, using the drawings inside to try to identify what they were seeing. Katherine found this exciting. For years it seemed she had lived with an awareness of these things but had never before discovered their use. She would often page through the books and pick out drawings and then show him where they were. Then together they would pour over the drawings and the objects until they discovered their function.

In one building they found an old vehicle that was shown in one of the books. It was a land vehicle that moved by itself. They spent the afternoon studying it, trying to find its source of power. Inside the front of it they found a tangle of rolling cord and metal pieces that Katherine said must be its energy, but Alovar, staring at it, could not understand how this could be so. What would feed it to make it move, and how did it move? How could metal and cord make something move from one point to another? The weight of it was such that Alovar could barely pick it up off the floor. He began to wonder if the drawings in the books were of real or imagined things. Katherine pointed out that so many of the objects and structures they had discovered in the books so far were real, why wouldn't all of them be the same?

Alovar could find no argument to counter this, and again went back to studying the books to try to divine what he could. He found a drawing with one of the land vehicles beside an obelisk. Running from the obelisk was a tube that flowed into the side of the vehicle. He became excited with this discovery and quickly showed it to Katherine. Together they poured over the pages, finding other objects like the one hooked up to the vehicle. In most of the drawings they found it hooked up in the same way. They decided finally that this thing must feed the vehicle somehow. Neither of them had the faintest idea how this could come about, but they were satisfied that they had finally figured out one mystery.

In a half-standing building they found one of the portable weapons used by the ancient people. It was covered with a fine yellowish mold that they scraped away until the metal emerged. Its parts no longer moved but Alovar, using the books, soon discovered how it must have worked. He didn't understand why it worked, but he knew now how it could shoot things out of its mouth. They took turns carrying it throughout the day, and often they would find their hands closing, without their awareness, over the handle of it. Neither of them liked the false strength it seemed to bring and they left it in one of the hidden rooms beneath the buildings, both of them beginning to understand that maybe the mere fact of having such weapons would lead people to use them.

Alovar found himself noticing Katherine more each day. He would often rise early and wait impatiently for her to show herself, looking forward to his first sight of her. He grew to know her face and her expressions. The sight of her smile made him smile.

Sometimes he would catch her looking thoughtfully out over the city, seemingly far away from him and their explorations, and he would wonder about these thoughts of hers and what they hid. He forced himself not to question her, but found this more and more difficult.

By the fire at dusk, each holding a mug of tea, they would sit silently, comfortable in their companionship. Alovar glanced at her, aware of her gaze. He ignored it, tightening his grip on his mug, letting its warmth seep through his callused hand.

"The Marauders killed them," she said abruptly.

Alovar looked at her, then away.

"We lived in the Realm," she said, "until my brother was born. He was damaged and they told us that he must be sent away. My mother would not do this." She paused, sipping her tea and looking deep into the fire.

Alovar watched her, thinking her words were spoken as if he wasn't there. It was as if they needed to be said, regardless of whether someone was there to listen or not. He wondered if she said them when she was alone. Did she sit by herself, where ever she camped, and speak these things to the night?

"My father said, 'This is the Realm, this is civilization. If we cannot act civilized, then we cannot be a part of the Realm.' My mother said, 'No, he is our son. How can we send him away to die?' My father wouldn't listen to her. He was ashamed that this had happened, that our neighbors should see this thing he had sown. He came to me that night and pleaded with me to make my mother see sense, to act in a civilized manner. I was only a child. I didn't know how to respond. I didn't know what life was, civilized or uncivilized."

She paused, then shifted closer to the fire. Alovar stood and placed a blanket around her shoulders. She clutched it tightly to her neck, her eyes fixed, seemingly unaware of his gesture. She spoke again.

"The next morning they came for us and told us either the mutant left or we all left. My father stood with them and watched as my mother came out of our house, carrying my brother. She said nothing. She looked at each of them, then settled her gaze on my father. He made no attempt to avoid her look. He was the first to step forward to take the baby. When she wouldn't release him, he turned and shrugged, as if telling the rest of them there was nothing more he could do. They led her to the border and waited for her to leave. My father waited with them. He stood beside me with his hand on my shoulder. I watched my mother turn away and walk across the sand. Never once had she said anything, and even then she walked away with pride."

Alovar refilled her mug, looking at her closely, trying to find some hint of emotion, but her face was impassive and gave away nothing.

"She had gone only a little way when my brother began to cry," she said, resuming her story as if she had never stopped. "One of the men standing next to my father laughed. When I turned to see who had done it, I noticed my father was smiling as well. I don't know if it was the laugh, the smile, or the cry that decided me, but one moment I was standing beside him and the next I was running across the sand to join my mother. I think I heard my father call out to me, but I wasn't sure and I never turned to see."

"For me it was much the same," he said. "They stripped me and stood watching as I left." Alovar sighed, remembering, amazed that he had felt he was being cast out from civilized society.

"I went only a short way before I first encountered the Marauders. I have learned since then that they wait on the outskirts of the Realm, they wait and prey on those who have been exiled." He looked across at her.

"They do," she nodded. "They were waiting for us. I was too young then, but my mother wasn't. When they were done with her, they left us. Long after they had disappeared from sight, I could still hear them laughing."

"That was a long time ago," Alovar offered, seeing the sudden stiffness in her posture.

"Sometimes I can close my eyes and still hear their laughter," Katherine said, looking across the fire at him.

"My mother cleaned herself, took my brother in her arms, and we began to walk again. It took us eight days to reach this city. We ran into three other bands of Marauders and each time it was the same. My mother never cried, she never said a word, or even tried to fight them, and I hated her. I hated the way she submitted. It was only later that I realized if she had done anything else, they would have killed us."

"Your mother was very strong."

"Yes," Katherine said.

Alovar sensed there was more.

"When we came to this city, I wanted nothing to do with her. I would sleep, dreaming about returning to the Realm. It was where I belonged, I thought, not with a foolish woman who would not even attempt to protect herself. I began to hate my brother, too. Each day I would watch him grow a little stronger, and I would hate the sight of his deformities, knowing that it was he who had driven us to this empty place."

"What did your mother say to you?" Alovar asked gently.

"She said nothing. She knew what I thought but refused to speak of it."

Alovar stoked the fire, then shifted his blanket to his shoulders. He bundled it beneath his neck, trying to hide from the evening chill.

"We stayed for four seasons. The third season my mother began to teach me. She taught me about civilization and being civilized. She showed me what these things meant. I grew to understand her and allowed myself to see my brother for what he was. He was not his deformity, that was only a part of him that was beyond his ken. It had no more bearing on who he was than the color of his hair. We made a place for ourselves and began to believe that life could exist out here in the burnt lands, that what was happening elsewhere did not have to occur here as well, that—" She stopped abruptly.

"What happened, Katherine?" Alovar asked gently.

Katherine ignored him and shifted to her side. She curled up beside the fire, covering herself with the blanket so that only the top of her head and eyes were revealed.

Alovar looked at her for a moment. Realizing that her story was finished, he threw more boards on the fire and curled up on his side. He could see her eyes reflected, darkly staring out at him.

Sleep eluded him. Each time he opened his eyes, he would see her staring blankly out at the night.

Later, as the embers had cooled and sleep began to finally descend on him, he thought he heard her speak once more.

"The Marauders came again, and this time I was not too young," he thought he heard her say, but wasn't sure if it was dream or real.

In the morning, when he woke and found her blanket wrapped around him, he remembered the words and still could not decide if he had dreamt them or not. He wondered if he would ever know for sure.

When she came for him later that morning, she acted as if nothing had been said the night before.

But as the day wore on, Alovar began to see how things had changed between them. It was a change that frightened him. It promised a great deal, but it was all in promises that Alovar did not know if he could honor. Not because he didn't want to. Because he didn't know if he knew how.

CHAPTER
14

STANDING ON MY porch, I watch the sun highlight the path leading up the hill from the gate. It reassures me to see it, to know that soon Katherine will be walking that path. I grin, baring teeth to the chill of the morning. A cloud of condensed breath floats out in front of me. Soon winter will come and the thought of it disturbs me. I don't know what it will mean in terms of Katherine. Will she still be able to visit?

I turn my thoughts away from this and back to the night before. I had the dream again, only this time, and it shouldn't have surprised me, when I answered the door it was Katherine standing there. We looked at each other for a moment, and then she smiled and did the most amazing thing. She stepped up to me and hugged me. I could actually feel her arms around me. They felt like nothing I had ever imagined. It was so potent that it woke me, and in that one moment between waking and sleep, I could feel her body still pressed against mine.

I stayed awake for hours, remembering, holding the memory of it as close as she had held me.

I glance at the stack of wood to the side and growl. The thought of gathering wood is not a pleasant one. It's a chore that I have to constantly force myself to do. It seems as if no sooner does winter end than I have to start the process all over again.

I head out behind the cabin. A hundred yards back, I take down a birch tree, then drag it into the front yard, where I begin to cut and split it down to stove size. It takes most of the morning to accomplish. By the time I'm done, I have a stack chest height across the front of the porch. The clean smell of birch fills the air. I inhale it, then scamper around to the back of the cabin and shower, paying close attention to the more odoriferous parts of my body.

A half an hour later, carefully combed and groomed, I hunker down against the wall of the cabin, contentedly rubbing the knobs of my spine against the wood, and wait for the sound of Katherine's car.

She comes almost every day now. She missed only once last week, and that time the old woman came up. It was strange seeing her after so long. She looked so old to me. I hadn't noticed that before. Seeing her hobble down the path made me suddenly ashamed of the way I had been treating her. Maybe some of this has to do with what Katherine's been telling me, maybe some of it has to do with my own age. Either way, I found myself feeling closer to her than I had in years.

I could tell the chair pleased her, though she didn't say much about it. That's always been the way with us, we rarely tell each other much of what we are feeling. I think we both know how difficult that would be, how much pain we might unleash.

I know and have always known that she is ashamed of me. My body embarrasses her. I am her son and her responsibility, and I guess I should be grateful that she has accepted both. Something he never could.

I walked her back along the path to her car, going slowly to keep pace with her. Her leg, she told me, would soon be as good as new, and I nodded and said that I was glad, remembering how it had happened. I glanced over at her and saw that same memory clouding her own thoughts. I wonder how often it comes to her? Does she remember the bite of the ax, the face of death above her?

At the gate she paused, then opened her arms to me. It was a familiar embrace long absent from my life. When she released me, she turned quickly to leave, but not fast enough for me to miss the sudden wash of moisture in her eyes.

"Be careful, Eddie," she said, then climbed into her car and drove down the hill.

I stayed until she was out of sight, thinking about her last words. It seems to me, I have always been careful. I have kept myself hidden from everyone. Even my arrangement with John is so convoluted and circumspect, he could never discover who I am. Edward Talbot, I have written him, is a pseudonym. He thinks she is the author of the Alovar books—Ann Talbot. The checks and royalties are in her name. I don't exist. I have no birth certificate.

There is no official evidence of my existence whatsoever. When I die, it will be as if I've never lived. And for a long time, I have felt as if this would not be far from the truth. It has only been recently that things have changed. For the first time in my life I have felt there was more to life than my books and the woods around me, and I know this is what the old woman was speaking about.

I light a cigarette and try to understand this. Before Katherine, things were what they were. There wasn't anything that could be done about it. I lived because I lived. I didn't particularly enjoy it, but I didn't hate it. It was all I knew and it was enough. To end it would have required a certain despondent energy that I didn't feel capable of manufacturing. Which was certainly not to say that I would never feel that way. In truth, I have always thought that eventually this would be my choice. It seemed only logical that it would happen.

The old woman would grow old and soon be unable to make the trips to the cabin. Finding someone to take on this chore would be next to impossible, especially once they discovered what their efforts were nourishing. It was an end that I had fully accepted. I had even spent time thinking about the ways I could possibly do it. If I was forced to live my life in seclusion, I absolutely refused to be displayed after my death. I would not want my body found.

After toying with various measures, I had decided that I would simply cut my wrists. I would wait until near unconsciousness and then set the cabin on fire. I am a complete coward when it comes to pain, and the thought of burning to death is not a particularly pleasant one. The fire, I felt quite sure, would destroy all but my bones, and the bones themselves, if they were ever even studied, would be attributed to some animal. No one would ever think that they were the skeletal structure of a man and, in some ways, they would be right.

What kind of a man lives his life in hiding, regardless of the boundaries of his prison? I have hidden quite successfully from all but a feeble old woman, who had the dubious distinction of being my mother. What kind of man is this, I wonder disgustedly, whose only accomplishment is to remain hidden? It isn't fair, I think. Then, thinking this, I begin to laugh.

My laughter howls out over my yard, and off in the distance, tears dripping from the corner of my eyes, I see a flock of crows take flight, fleeing the sound. The sight of this sobers me.

I absently run my hand along my chest, smoothing down the hair. I glance down, noticing a splash of white hair in the middle of my breast bone. I think it makes me look quite distinguished and wish for a moment I had a mirror, an object that I had long ago decided was superfluous.

I rise to my feet, stretch hugely, and bare my teeth to the sky. Inhaling, I can smell the scent of winter. The trees are almost all denuded. Soon the snow will come, a time of year that has never been my favorite.

I think about it now, and imagine myself standing in front of my cook stove with a book, or bowed over my desk working on Alovar, and in each of these positions I'm not alone. Someone sits with me. We talk and listen to the silence of the snow and feel the heat from the fire. We—

I prick my ears at a distant sound. A moment later comes the steady rumble of Katherine's car.

I stub out my cigarette and race down the hill towards the gate. Safely hidden behind the brambles of a holly tree, I wait for Katherine to arrive. I wonder what she'll be wearing, and look forward to telling her about the woman Alovar has met. I wonder if I should tell her the name.

"It's getting cold," she says, as we climb up the path together, or as together as we can be.

"Yes, it will snow soon."

"What'll you do in the winter?" she asks, pausing to look over in my direction.

"Same thing I always do."

"Does Annie come up to see you as often?" she asks, resuming her pace.

"As much as she can. Usually we try to make sure that I'm well stocked with canned goods and other imperishables."

"Sounds pretty bleak."

"It's not too bad. I have my books and Alovar," I tell her, wondering if I should say anything about the other Katherine.

"Seems like there should be more than that," she says softly.

I grunt.

"Don't start that again."

"Yes."

At the top of the hill she pauses to catch her breath.

I watch her lean over at the waist, drawing in deep breaths. She's wearing the frayed jeans this time. My favorites. Bent over the way she is, they conform to her butt quite enticingly.

"Don't you ever get out of breath?" she pants.

"Not too much."

"Jesus," she says, shaking her head in amazement. "With all the smoking you do, I would have thought you'd be coughing and hacking all the time."

I inhale deeply, testing myself for any incipient coughs. The lungs feel as good as ever. I exhale, glancing off to the west, wondering how far away the rabbit is. Lately, it seems to me, there have been more animals than usual coming around the cabin. I'm not sure if this my own imagination or what. It's been a long time since this has happened, and I enjoy the thought that maybe I have been forgiven for that brief spell of behavior. It's still a time that shames me, but I find it a much less potent memory than it has been before.

"Did you hear that?" Katherine suddenly asks.

"The squirrel?" I answer.

"You heard a squirrel?"

"Yes."

"I didn't hear that. I was talking about the jay."

"Oh, yes, the jay."

"What else did you hear?"

"When?"

"Just now."

"Things."

"What kind of things?"

"Lots of things."

"Edward," she warns.

"I heard a squirrel, the rustling of a rabbit, the sound of the leaves falling, and off by the cabin I think I left the shower dripping."

"You're kidding?"

"No."

"You heard a leaf falling?"

"Didn't you?"

"Jesus Christ, what kind of ears do you have?"

I reach up and smooth back my left ear; it pops right back up and points towards her.

"They aren't like mine are they?" she asks a moment later, glancing over in my direction.

This is unfamiliar ground for me. I grunt.

"Are we back to the burn explanation?" she asks disparagingly.

"It would seem so," I say judiciously, finding it almost as ridiculous as she does.

She's discovered enough about me, through our conversations, to know that the "burn explanation" is completely apocryphal.

"Why don't you just tell me about it," she asks, then begins to walk again.

I trail along in the woods, darting from tree to tree, thinking about this. I finally decide to venture a small part of the truth to see what will happen.

"I wasn't burned."

"No kidding," she says sarcastically, without the faintest appreciation of my honesty.

We walked a few yards without speaking.

"Are you pouting?" she asks.

"No."

"Sounds like you are."

"I'm not."

"Yes, you are."

"No, I'm not."

"You are."

"I'm not."

"Are."

"Not."

"*Are,*" she sings out, one last time, then dances on ahead of me up the path.

I catch up to her and walk alongside in the woods, trying to decide what I can tell.

"You know," she says, "rather than trying to come up with a good story, why don't you just try the truth."

It surprise me that she can so easily read my thoughts. It also pleases me, but this is something I will save to consider later this evening.

"It can't be that bad, Edward. Why don't you just tell me about it?"

I walk for a few more feet and then say, "It wasn't any

accident, at least not in the accepted connotations of the word."

"Are you going to get all booky on me."

"What do you mean, 'booky'?"

"I mean, whenever you talk about yourself, about the personal stuff, you start getting all pompous. Can't you just talk like you usually do?"

I consider this for a moment and find myself wanting to argue about it. The only thing that stops me is that I know she's right. I do have a tendency to abstract myself with words. It's something I have noticed before. With the old woman I don't do this, but with Katherine I find myself at times saying things that even I have trouble understanding.

"So, you going to tell me or what?" she asks.

"It wasn't an accident," I begin, then pause for a moment, not quite sure how to follow this.

"You were born this way?" she prompts.

"Yes." I answer, breathing out the word like a gout of smoke.

Katherine continues walking. She stares at the ground before her. I notice her hand has risen to her forehead where it plays with a shock of her hair. It's a gesture I'm quite familiar with, it's something she always does when she's thinking. The consolation in this, I realize, is that Katherine always seems to tell me what she thinks. Her thoughts flow right from her brain to her tongue. I admire this about her. My own thoughts are rarely this clear. Only when I'm writing do they flow this easily.

"Did you ever see a doctor about it?"

"No. The old woman told me the doctor who delivered me said nothing could be done."

"Be done about what?" she asks.

"About me."

"About you how? Do you have extra fingers, webbed feet? What're we talking about here?"

"Katherine," I say, "if that's all it was, I wouldn't live the way I do."

"So, it's worse." Her hand rises to her forehead.

"Yes. It is."

"How much worse?"

"More than you can imagine probably."

"I think what I imagine is probably much worse than you could ever possibly be," she says, looking towards the woods.

I shake my head and answer, "You think I won't be as horrid as you imagine, when in all truth, I'm far more."

"That's not true, Edward."

"Yes, it is," I say, and race through the woods towards my cabin. I rush inside and pull the curtains.

By the time she appears on the crest of the hill, I am leaning against the door frame watching her. The sun enjoys her. It splashes brightly all around her and seems to highlight her features and luminescent hair. It makes her more beautiful and she is already the most beautiful thing I have ever seen.

"I read it," she tells me, lounging on the other side of the door across the porch.

"Oh. . . ."

"That's all you have to say?"

"Yes," I answer, then suddenly add, "look at that, that cloud over there."

"That's not going to work, Edward," she tells me, without even glancing toward the sky."

"Oh."

"It's you, isn't it? The son?"

"Every writer incorporates parts of himself into his books," I say, somewhat pompously.

"We're not talking about other writers here, we're talking about you, and it is you, isn't it?"

"A part of me," I grudgingly admit.

"Was your father that bad?"

"He was bad."

"How bad? As bad as in the book?"

Was he that bad? I wonder, remembering the way he stood in the attic, staring at me, never speaking, ax in hand, the old woman screaming on the steps, and suddenly the feel of the ax in my own hands. No, I think, he wasn't that bad. He was much worse.

"Was he?" Katherine asks again.

"He was terrible, Katherine. But he's dead now, and what he did and what he thought doesn't matter."

She accepts this, yet I can sense that it is only for the moment.

"The ending was pretty bleak," she says.

"I didn't think it was that bleak."

"You destroyed the world. That's pretty bleak."

"If the world was as I had portrayed it, it should have been destroyed."

"Do you believe that?"

"Yes."

"You think you'd have that right, if you felt things were that bad?"

"Yes. Don't people have that right now? Aren't there men in Washington who can do exactly that?"

"But they're supposedly bound by laws and regulations

that forbid them to do it on their own. No one man can determine the fate of the world or the country." She pauses, then adds, "I don't think anyone can make that kind of decision."

"It was only fiction."

"I wonder," she says thoughtfully, smoothing back her hair.

I make coffee, and when she's not looking, open the door a crack and place it on the porch. Beside it I put two Oreo cookies and a napkin.

"You know I hate these things," she says.

"What?"

"These cookies. I don't know how you can stand them. They make your mouth black."

I glance down at the black saliva dripping on my chest and have to agree with her.

"You ever try Pepperidge Farm Italian Thins?"

"No."

"Next trip, I'll bring some up," she says, and as soon as she mentions this, I find myself wondering what she's brought this time.

I scrutinize her closely but can't discern any packages or bulges in her clothes, other than the ones I've already examined minutely, and I know that they belong only to her.

She seems to sense my curiosity, for she says, "I brought you something different today."

"What?" I ask, unable to hide my excitement.

She laughs. "You'll just have to wait. I'll give it to you later."

"What is it?"

"Be patient, I'll give it to you."

"Is it sweet or spicy?" I ask.

She shakes her head.

"Small or large?"

"Edward," she cautions, "wait."

I pop a cookie into my mouth.

"May I have some more coffee?" she asks, putting her cup by the door.

I open the door and pull the cup inside. At the stove I refill it, baring my teeth, thinking about the difficulty we had in accomplishing this arrangement of refreshments. At first she had absolutely refused to turn her back while I put out her coffee. "What possible harm can it do for me to see your hand?" she would ask, and I glanced down at the knobby, heavily nailed appendage at the end of my arm, and said, "You'd be surprised." Finally she had agreed.

I turn away from the stove to see the door slowly being opened.

"Katherine!" I shout, and the door pauses, barely opened, but enough so that she could easily slip her head through.

For a moment we both seem frozen. I can see her fingertips around the edge of the door, her scent bathes the cabin, the fresh odor of soap and perfume, and beneath it a pungent excitement, a smell that frightens me.

"It'll be all right, Edward," she says. "Please, it won't matter what you look like."

"Katherine, go back outside," I say, more calmly than I feel, sensing her indecision, fearing her response if she steps through the door.

It seems to take forever for the door to slowly close. I exhale, then glance down at my hands. Coffee has spilled from each of the cups. It takes a long time before the shaking stops.

I glance out the window to see her sitting with her arms wrapped around her knees, her chin resting on her forearms as she stares at the woods.

I put the coffee outside the door, then close and lock it.

"I heard that," she says softly. "You don't have to lock it. I won't do it again, unless you want me to." There is a moment's silence. "Will you ever want me to?"

I am not sure how to answer her. What I want and what I can have are such complete opposites that I can't ever imagine them coinciding.

We sip our coffee together, separated by the wall of the cabin.

"My uncle's been asking me again about where I go."

"What do you tell him?"

"What I always tell him—exploring."

"Does he believe you?"

"No. He thinks I have a boyfriend."

"And what do you say when he says that?"

"I tell him . . . that maybe I do."

She turns to stare at my window. I blush and step back, grunting softly to myself. I paw the floor.

"What are you doing in there?"

"Nothing," I manage to squeak out, wanting to howl at the top of my lungs, wanting to hear my voice echo through the trees in a shriek of victory. It's absolutely absurd, but when I'm with her—talking—I think everything is possible.

"He tried to follow me today," she says, and it takes a moment for me to hear this. When I do, I grab the curtain and stare out at her.

"I lost him on the back roads."

I try to imagine what this means but can't.

"I don't know what I'm going to do about him. I'm going

to have to either tell him something, or not come up here for a while."

I listen to this and can't imagine it. I don't want to go back to the silence, the absolute emptiness of the cabin and the woods.

"What do you think I should do?" she says.

I say the only thing I can think to say: "I don't want you to go away."

She turns, smiles.

Looking at her smile, I find I don't care about any of it, her uncle, the old woman, or any of them down below.

"Okay, then," she says. "I'll work something out. But you have to promise me, Edward."

"What?"

"That you'll think about me. That you'll think about letting me see you. It can't be so bad that I won't be able to see beyond it."

"Katherine. . . . Do you think I would live this way if it wasn't?"

"But how awful can it be?" she cries, rising to her feet and coming to my window.

I move back and see her shadow before the curtain.

"Edward? How terrible can it possibly be?" she cries, pressing her face to the window, her shadow in silhouette across the curtain.

I try to find words to tell her. I can't seem to voice them. How can I describe what I am, when even I don't fully realize the extent in comparison with everyone else. I've lived alone so long that whatever travesty of a normal human existence I might have retained, from my years with the old woman, have been lost. I live my life according to what makes me comfortable, and my comfort is fully dependent on the grotesque angles and awkward lines of my body. I can remember only the horror in his eyes, when he would stand and watch me. The old woman's reflect only her sense of herself in relation to me. Those are the only eyes in which I've ever seen myself reflected.

"Please, Katherine."

She steps away from the window, back across the porch, down to the front yard. I watch her stand over the tulip bed.

"They won't come up until spring," she says. "Will I get to see you then, Edward? Will I get to see what you look like next spring, or maybe next summer, or even next winter? When do I get to see you, Edward? Don't you understand that it doesn't matter? That what I . . ." She looks away.

"Katherine," I call to her, but she refuses to turn. "Katherine," I call again.

She turns, but refuses to look towards the cabin.

I see the line of her scalp and take the scent of her deep into my lungs. I hold both of these inside, scarring myself with them, until they will always be a part of me.

"I have to go," she sniffles.

"It's still early."

"No, I should get going before my uncle gets worried."

"What are you going to tell him?"

"I'll tell him to leave me alone."

"Will he do that?"

"I don't know," she says, then turns and begins to walk up the path.

I race out the door and into the woods.

We walk silently towards the gate. As we approach it, she stops and looks towards the woods.

I call to her to let her know where I am.

"This is what I brought you," she says, taking out a

crumpled piece of tissue paper and placing it on the path. "I want you to have this," she says, then turns away.

At the gate, she adds, "You'll know what to do with it," then turns and climbs into her car and drives away.

I wait until her car disappears over the hill before I race out onto the path and to the paper lying there. I pick it up, sniffing at it curiously. I pick up her scent but nothing else. I wonder what this could be, then open it up.

Inside, wrapped carefully in tissue paper, is a ring. It's one I've often seen on her finger. I asked her about it once and she told me it was her grandmother's, and that it was the only thing she had ever been given by anyone that she wanted to keep.

I hear the fading sound of her car in the distance and carefully pick up the ring. It fits over the nail of my little finger, but goes no farther. Staring at its delicate design, looking at it hanging haphazardly over my grubby fingernail, I have the absurd desire to weep.

I howl instead, and hear the scampering sounds of every animal within earshot trying to race away.

I continue to howl long after the sound of their retreat has died, until my lungs hurt and my chest heaves with the effort.

I carry the ring reverently in my closed hand, holding it tightly to my chest, and lope back to the cabin. Blood drips from my lower lip. Some of it splashes across my closed fist.

Back at the cabin, I notice a small stain of blood, dried and cracked, on the surface of the ring. I rub it away carefully, then clasp my hand tightly.

Later I string it on a cord that I loop around my neck, so I can always look down to see it.

I fall asleep that night holding it, and dream my usual dream. I wake, again with the feel of Katherine's arms around me, and drift back to sleep, holding her ring.

CHAPTER
15

I LIMPED TO the hardware store this afternoon and overheard two men talking. One of them was a stranger and the other I have seen around town. He had on a Mobil gas station shirt with the name *Josh* stitched across the pocket. The stranger was asking him who lived up in the cabin by Flag Mountain. Hearing that, I froze, and waited to hear what would come next.

"Didn't know anybody had a place up that way," Josh answered.

"Saw a car up there by a gate, a yellow Volkswagen. Didn't see anybody around, but must be someone up there," the stranger replied. I peeked over the aisle.

"Know the car," Josh said, "don't know who else might be up there. Thought that was California people that owned that place," he said thoughtfully, then went on to talk about hunting.

I left without buying anything and hurried home, trying to figure out what to do. I knew Josh would mention it to someone.

Jake's been after me again about his niece, wondering all the time where she goes off to so much.

I have to let Eddie know what's going on. What to tell him? Maybe he'll have an idea. Seems to me, the only thing we can do is go away for a while and hope everything blows over. If it doesn't, we'll just have to leave for somewhere else. I hate the thought of that. I've come to think of this place as home. Leaving it would be hard. But not leaving might be a whole lot harder.

Wrapped my knee real good and thought if I took it easy it'd be okay. I was just about out the door, to go see Eddie, when I saw Jake arrive.

"Annie," he said. "Where you think you're going? You know you shouldn't be walking around with that leg of yours the way it is."

I told him I was just going down to the store to pick up some items.

He told me to sit right back down and he'd get them for me. I sat down, figuring I'd get rid of him as soon as I could. I didn't know what else to do. It was still early enough so I could make the trip and be back before dark.

I made up a list and sent him off. Seemed like I just sat there staring at the clock, wanting him to get back. Took him almost an hour before he returned carrying two bags of groceries. Why had I given him such a long list.

"Now you just sit down and I'll put these things away for you," he said, winking at me and stepping right into the kitchen. Seemed like he was in there forever before I called out to ask him what he was doing. "Nothing," he called back, and stayed out there.

Finally I went to see what was going on. He was standing

at the stove humming to himself. When he heard me, he turned, smiling like he'd just eaten the canary.

"What're you doing out here?" I said, maybe a bit more sharply than I meant to.

It didn't seem to bother him any; he just kept smiling.

"Well, I thought since you weren't feeling so good, I'd make you up some lunch."

I almost groaned out loud. Seemed like it took him forever to get it ready. By the time he brought it out to me, it was almost one-thirty. Took us another hour or so to eat it. While we were eating, he asked me again about Kat, asked me if I'd seen her lately.

I told him that no, I hadn't seen her in quite a while, which was a lie. I'd just seen her the other day. She's the only one I have to talk to about Eddie. As much as I don't like the idea of the two of them spending so much time together, it's nice sharing Eddie with her.

"I don't know where she's been going, Annie. I think maybe she's got herself someone." Jake was looking worried.

Made me feel sorry for him. I know all he's trying to do is to take care of her. I wished there was some way I could make him feel a little easier about it without hurting Eddie at the same time.

"What's wrong with that?" I asked. "She's a pretty enough girl, once you get by that hair of hers. Doesn't seem like that'd be too bad of a thing."

"Well, you know," he said, "I'm supposed to be looking out for her while she's with me. I don't mind that she got herself someone she's seeing, but what bothers me is that she won't tell me anything about him. It would seem to me, if this was a nice enough young man, she wouldn't have any trouble bringing him around so I could meet him."

What could I say to that? Wasn't anything I could say. I just nodded, wishing he would leave.

He did all the dishes, then came back and sat with me for a while longer in the parlor. It wasn't until a little after four before he finally left.

I almost went up to Eddie's then, but knew if I did I was only taking a chance on busting up the van or hurting myself trying to get up that track of his. I figured I could wait at least one more day, without it mattering too much.

Then Marilyn called and wanted to talk about church again. I couldn't help myself; I didn't want to hear any of that stuff. I told her that flat out. I could tell it shocked her, because right after that she asked me if I was feeling all right. I told her I was feeling just fine, but a little on the busy side right then. She hung up, hurt, but what else could I tell her?

The next morning, at first light, I set out.

Eddie came down to meet me and, as soon as I got through the gate, I started telling him what I heard at the hardware store. When I was finished, Eddie just looked down at me, walking beside him, and asked, "Your leg okay?"

"*Forget* my leg!" I shouted at him. "Didn't you hear what I was just telling you?"

"Of course I did, but I notice you're limping quite a bit."

"It doesn't hurt that much. It's just being cramped up in the car is all," I said, feeling a little put out that he wasn't taking this more seriously.

"Here, why don't you lean on me," he said, offering me his shoulder.

I tried to lean on him, but he's so big it didn't do no good at all. Seemed like, if anything, it hurt more that way.

Finally he just scooped me up in his arms and carried me up to the cabin. I kept looking at him, trying to figure out what he was thinking. I could tell he was. I know him well enough to be able to see that in him. But he sure wasn't saying anything.

He put me down in my chair and poured us each a coffee.

"Well," I said, "what're we going to do?"

"About what?"

"About the car being seen. Don't you think people are going to start to wonder about that?"

"They've seen cars before."

"But they never seen a woman's car before."

"So, what difference does that make?"

Only realizing that he was absolutely serious, kept me from yelling at him right then. I keep forgetting that Eddie doesn't know about people and how people will always think the worst.

"Eddie," I said, trying to be as gentle as I could. "No one knows about you living up here, and that's good, and even if they thought there was someone living up here, they might be a little curious, but the fence and all would keep them away. They'd just think you wanted to be alone and they'd let you have that."

"So what's the problem then?" he said, furrowing his brow until the hair seemed to completely cover his eyes.

I always used to think that made him look kind of cute, but right then I wasn't too good at seeing cute.

"The problem is, is now there's a girl, a town girl. Don't matter that she's just visiting. She's a relative of one of the locals, and they're all going to be wondering who's messing around with her."

"We're not messing around," Eddie said, baring his teeth at me.

"Don't you be doing that to me," I warned, reaching out and swatting him across the arm. "This is serious. There's going to be people who are going to start asking questions about who's living back here. Only a matter of time before someone comes up to see for himself what's going on."

Eddie stalked over to the window and looked out.

"You understand what I'm saying to you?" I said sharply.

"Yes."

"Then I think we should get out of here for a while. Just until things blow over, then we'd come back and see what's happening."

"The land is in your name. Why don't you just tell them something."

"What am I going to tell them?"

"Tell them you told Katherine she could come up here," he said, turning to look at me.

"What if they don't believe me?"

"Why wouldn't they?" He looked at me curiously.

I didn't much like the way he was looking. "Why're you looking at me like that?"

"You want me to stop seeing her, don't you?" he said.

I couldn't deny that, and for a moment wondered if that was what I was doing, but it wasn't like that. This whole thing was giving me a bad feeling and I tried to describe that to Eddie, but he wouldn't listen to me.

"I'm not going to do that," he said, then added a moment later, "I can't do that."

"Eddie?"

"No, you just tell them she's taken up hiking and she's got your permission."

"People are going to wonder. People don't let things like this go."

"Things like what? People are always hiking around this area. It's not going to surprise anyone," Eddie said.

I could tell, looking at him, that he'd already made up his mind, but I couldn't let it go. I could feel it going wrong and kept trying to explain that to him. He refused to even listen to me.

"You never liked my seeing her. You always thought it was wrong. Well, it isn't. We like each other."

I noticed the way his hand kept going to his chest. I saw the cord, half buried in the hair, and what was hanging at the end of it. Eddie noticed what I was looking at and bared his teeth.

"She gave me this," he said, coming over to show me.

He was like a little boy, crouching before me with a new treasure. I grabbed the ring and ripped it from his neck.

"You *got* to listen to me, Eddie! This isn't going to turn out good." I was screaming.

He stared at me for a long time, then held out his hand. "Give it back to me," was all he said.

I handed it back and watched him tie it in place. He came over and lifted me up, carried me out the door and headed back down the path. We didn't say nothing to each other. I didn't know what else to say, and I could tell by the set of his jaw that he wasn't going to listen anyway.

"Will you at least think about what I said?" I asked him. "Will you think about Kat?"

"What about Katherine?"

"Think about what it'd be like for her if something happened to you." For the first time, I saw my words getting through to him. Maybe I shouldn't have added what I said next, but how could I help it? "And what about me, think about what it would be like for me."

He looked at me in the oddest way.

"You're my son, I love you," I said, and suddenly found

myself trying to remember the last time I had said it to him. It shamed me that I couldn't.

Eddie didn't reply. He just kept moving steadily down to the gate.

I drove away without saying anything else to him. In the side mirror I could see him standing there by the gate, watching me go.

When I got home I called Kat and told her I had to see her. She said she was on her way to Eddie, and I said to forget that and come over first. She finally agreed to, for just a little while.

"What, what is it?" she asked, after she'd stepped inside and sat down.

"Your uncle's been asking me about you again."

"What'd you tell Jake?" she asked, looking all worried. It surprised me that she might think I would ever tell him about Eddie. I don't know how things got to be like this, all of a sudden.

"I told him I didn't know where you were going."

She smiled.

I said, "I just went up to see Eddie." Her smile disappeared. Then I told her about what I'd heard down at the hardware store. When I was done, she just looked at me and shrugged.

"So," she said.

"Kat!" I was trying to be patient with her, thinking maybe she didn't quite understand what was going on here. "If people go up that way, they're bound to find Eddie. If that should come about, what'd you think's going to happen?"

"I don't really know," she said, and couldn't help the smile.

"Jesus, girl, think! Think what that would mean," I said, probably a little louder than I should have.

"Might mean that he could stop hiding," she said.

I glanced at her, thinking she was crazy, and then I realized that she'd never seen Eddie. She didn't have the faintest idea what I was talking about.

"You don't know, do you?"

"About him, you mean?"

"Yes, about what he looks like."

"He won't let me see him," she said, "but I think he's going to, soon."

"Kat," I said, sitting down beside her and taking her hands in mine. "It's not what you think it is. This isn't some fairy tale where everyone's going to live happily ever after. Eddie's hiding because he has to hide. People wouldn't understand if they saw him."

"He can't be that gruesome, Annie. I've talked to him."

"Talking to him and seeing him are two different things."

"If he can just talk to people, then they'll understand him."

I shook my head at her, thinking how young she was, how little she understood. "Folks aren't going to let him talk. They're going to see him and they're going to hurt him." I was trying to make her believe me.

She wouldn't.

"Annie, I don't think normal people act that way. They aren't going to just . . . attack him because of what he looks like," she said, smiling at me and pushing herself to her feet.

"He tell you about Ted?" I asked, as she started for the door. She stopped and turned.

"He didn't, did he?" I said, feeling my knee start to ache, feeling so tired that I didn't know if I could get the words out.

"He didn't tell you what happened, how his father died?" I saw it all again, the bite of the ax, the howl coming out of Eddie's mouth—like nothing I had ever heard before or wished I'd ever hear again.

When she sat back down, I told her about it, about how it had been.

"He hated Eddie. I didn't know that, though God knows I should have. I just always thought he didn't quite know what to do with the boy. Later, after it had all happened, and after some of the things Eddie told me, I realized that it was right there to see, if I had cared to look. I guess I just didn't want to. It was easier thinking everything would turn out all right. Seemed like everything else was in such a mess that something had to be all right.

"Ted never even talked to him. Only time he did was the day he died, and what he said to him then wasn't much in the way of talking.

"Ted . . . had killed the doctor that delivered Eddie. He told me the morning everything happened. You see, the doctor that delivered Eddie thought he was some kind of medical freak. He wanted to write him up in those medical journals. I didn't know about any of that at the time because I was still recovering from the birth. It was a hard birth. Took me almost twenty hours to bring that boy into the world and afterward there wasn't nothing that was going to take him away from me, not my husband or anyone else. But Ted, he didn't see it that way. All he saw was what Eddie looked like. He never could see beyond it. When he heard that doctor talking, all he could see was what they'd be saying about him. How it was his fault that Eddie was the way he was.

"Ted was a proud man. He couldn't have lived with that. I'm not trying to excuse him, I'm just telling you how he was.

Things had been good between us right up until the time Eddie was born, then everything just went bad.

"The doctor never had a chance to write his papers. No one even knew Edward was born. Never had no birth certificate. Only people who ever knew about him, was me, the doctor, the Reverend, Ted—and now you. That's it. Two of those people are dead, and one won't never mention it because he's so ashamed of himself. That leaves us two."

"You said Ted hated him," she asked.

I nodded. "The morning Ted finally told me about the doctor, he'd been drinking all night. The more he drank, the wilder he became. I kept waiting for him to pass out or something, but it never happened. He just kept getting crazier and crazier the more he drank. I could hear Eddie upstairs shifting around, and knew he could tell what was going on. I wanted to go up to him, to tell him everything was going to be all right, but I didn't want to leave Ted alone. I was afraid of what he was going to do to himself. I should've been more afraid for Eddie.

"Finally, about ten o'clock the next morning, Ted went upstairs into the attic. I started to follow him but he told me to just sit back down. He wanted to talked to the boy, alone. For a while I thought maybe it was going to be all right, maybe Ted had finally worked it all out and was going to try to reach out to him. I should have known. I should've known he wouldn't do nothing like that. . . ."

"What happened?" she said.

"You see, Ted used to go up to the attic most every day. It was only later that Eddie told me about this. He'd go up there whenever I left house, and then come right back down as soon he heard my car in the drive. Eddie told me he never said anything to him. He'd just stand there, staring at him for hours, smoking one cigarette after another, not saying a word. Eddie said, at first he tried to talk to him, but Ted wouldn't even nod to him. It got so Eddie just ignored him when he came up there. At least that's what Eddie says now, but I don't think it was like that. I think there was other things happening up there. It was the way Eddie looked when he told me all this, the way his eyes kept shifting around. The boy's never been much at lying, and having heard him talk about this, I could tell he was lying, though why, I don't know. It wouldn't matter much one way or the other. My feelings about Ted sure aren't going to change. He was a good man, once. But things just got to be too much for him.

"Ted went up to the attic and stopped in the side closet on the way. When he came back out he was carrying an ax. Least that's what I figured out later. I think that ax must have been there for a long time. I think that's what Ted was doing up there all those times when I wasn't around. I think he was looking at the boy, trying to work up the nerve to do something about him. That last day he finally managed to work up the nerve. I don't know why. I don't know what it was that finally set him off. I guess that's something I'll never know and can't say I really want to.

"I remember I was sitting in the kitchen, listening to Ted's footsteps climbing those stairs, thinking that it was going to be all right, that maybe Ted had finally come around. I don't know why I was thinking that. Maybe I was just as crazy as Ted then. Everything'd been so crazy for us for such a long time, seemed like I couldn't tell anymore what made sense and what didn't."

"Oh, Annie!"

"It was the screaming that made me realize how wrong I'd been. I could hear Ted up there, screaming at the top of his lungs. Then, the next moment, I heard this crash. Without even thinking about it, I raced up the stairs, not sure what I'd find, thinking one minute that something had happened to Ted and the next thinking something had happened to Eddie. There was even a time, God forgive me, that I found myself thinking that maybe Eddie'd gone crazy and become what he looked like.

I opened the door to the attic and saw Eddie rushing towards me with an ax in his hand. Ted was sprawled out across the floor behind him.

" '*Stop him,*' Ted screamed at me, and before I knew what I was doing, I put my hands up to stop Eddie from getting out.

"Eddie saw me standing that way and skidded to a stop. He was breathing hard, his teeth bared. I didn't know what was going on. Seeing Eddie that way, I guess I just thought the worst possible thing I could think.

"Eddie just stared at me for a second, then his face crumpled all up and his shoulders sagged like they were carrying half the world. He dropped the ax onto the floor and slowly bowed his head. Later, when I thought about it, I realized the reason he was acting that way was because he saw me standing there all set to stop him, as if I just naturally knew it was all his fault. It breaks my heart now. Eddie's the gentlest boy I've ever known. Why would I have thought . . . ?"

"What happened," Kate said.

"Ted started laughing. He was quicker than a snake. Snatched that ax right off the floor and lifted it over his head. I saw Eddie one instant before that ax started to fall. He just looked back at me, not making any move to get out of the way, just waiting for it to happen, like there was nothing else in the world he could do. It was that look that made me move.

"I shoved him out of the way, screaming. That ax came right down into my knee and knocked me across the floor.

Didn't hurt much at first. I remember looking down and seeing where this chunk of flesh had been gouged right out of my leg. It took a moment for the blood to start. When it did, it woke me up some. I glanced up to see Ted raising the ax again. Only this time he wasn't aiming at Eddie, he was aiming it at me."

"What'd you do?"

I could see Eddie behind him, and then the ax. I closed my eyes, waiting for it to happen, just like Eddie had done.

"There was a roar and the sound of the two of them colliding. When I opened my eyes, Ted was sprawled out across Eddie's chest. His hands were wrapped around Edward's throat, choking him to death. Eddie wasn't doing anything. He was just lying there, letting Ted do this thing. There wasn't any question about what would happen if Eddie tried to stop him. I knew how strong the boy was. He could have easily picked up Ted with one hand and thrown him clear across the room if he wanted to. But he didn't. He would've just let Ted kill him."

Kate's eyes were brimming with tears as she listened.

"What else could I do. There was nothing else. I had to. I got up and grabbed the ax. I didn't even aim it. I just swung it. I don't know what I was thinking then. I just wanted it all to end.

"The ax hit Ted in the back of the head. It near split his head wide open. That was the last thing I saw. The next thing I remember was being on the floor, listening to Eddie howl. It was like nothing I had ever heard before. Like it was torn right out of his guts."

"We never said nothing to anyone about it. A few months later Eddie's book got published. With that and the insurance money, we came out here."

"*The Abomination?*" Kate whispered.

"Yes," I nodded. "That's what Ted was screaming at him. Sitting on his chest, his hands around his neck, he just kept repeating that over and over again, spitting it into Eddie's face."

"Poor Edward," Kate said softly, glancing out the window.

"Poor Eddie," I agreed, and watched her.

When she turned back to me, she smiled, and then I knew I hadn't done any good.

"I have to go soon. It's almost too late for me to go up and back before dark."

"Kat, don't you understand what I just told you."

"But that was Ted's reaction, That isn't mine or anybody else's."

"No!" I said. "That's his father who did that. And if a person's father can't . . . then how can you expect anyone else to?"

She looked at me for a moment, then abruptly stood up and walked to the bookcase. She stood there.

"What does he look like? Just tell me that. What does he look like?"

I guess it was her anger that surprised me. I hadn't expected that, and it was such that it made me close my eyes. I didn't open them until I was done. I didn't want to watch what the words would do to her.

"He has teeth, and he has hair, though it's more fur than hair. His arms are twisted all backwards and bunched up with muscles. Both his legs are all bowed out, and his back isn't straight. It's got a hump in the center of it, and he can't sit down like everyone else. He has to always stand up or lie down on his side."

"What else?" she asked softly.

And all I could think was, Why does there have to be more? Why can't the boy be left alone? Why on earth do we have to do this thing to him? Why do we, the only two people who seem to know and care about him, have to be like this with each other?

"Sometimes, when he runs, he falls down on all fours. He's quick and can move through the woods like he belongs there. And sometimes, when he's upset or when he's excited, his teeth will cut into his lower lip and it'll start to bleed. . . ."

"No more. I don't want to hear any more."

"When he eats, he can't keep the food in his mouth 'cause his mouth is so twisted."

"Please, no more," Katherine pleaded.

"His ears are pointed like a dog's, they stand right up on either side of his head."

"Please! Annie!"

"His forehead juts out like those prehistoric men, and his eyes are set way back in his face. They're kind of a greenish brown, more like a cat's than anything else. And he's got. . . ."

"*No!*" Kate screamed and rushed at me.

What could I do but hold her and listen to her cry. All I can say is, she didn't cry alone.

My leg was aching something awful. I put some more of that salve on it, but it didn't seem to take away much of the pain. My arm was hurting me some, too. I don't know why. I didn't do anything to it that I can remember. Seemed stiff and numb, like it's been asleep. I keep trying to work the kinks out.

Maybe it wasn't fair, telling her those things, but it would have been more unfair not to. At least now she knows what's up there, what she thinks people'll understand. Hard to remember being that young, feeling so good about the world.

She left almost an hour later. Neither of us said much to each other after that. I guess we'd said everything we could say.

She didn't go up to see Eddie. I know that much. But what she's going to do tomorrow, I don't know.

CHAPTER

16

''IN THERE,'' SHE said, pointing.

To Alovar, the building looked no different than any of the others they had seen. One side of it was destroyed so that only three walls remained standing. The roof was torn off, leaving strips of jagged metal twisting into the air.

"By that corner," Katherine said, stepping carefully through the rubble.

Alovar paused for a moment to watch her, admiring her easy stride.

"See. It's just like the others," she said, stooping down to point.

Alovar examined the floor carefully before he saw the creases of the hidden door.

Katherine opened it and led him down to her camp.

A profusion of light! The light seemed almost brighter down below than it had been on the surface. Katherine led him to the southwest wall and showed him a metal grate that allowed the light to shine through. The light hit a wall of mirrors and splashed it all about the room.

Alovar marveled at the feel of the space, the sense of comfort it seemed to impart.

Katherine smiled at him and led him to another room, curtained off with a ground sheet. She pulled the sheet aside to show him what she had scavenged throughout the city and hidden there.

It was stacked with containers—cans. From bottom to top, rows of them gleamed in the mirrored sunlight. Alovar examined them in amazement. He had never seen such a bounty.

She nodded her assent and Alovar pulled down a can. On the front was a picture, and across the picture were the same kind of scribbles that he had seen in his paper books.

"The pictures," Katherine explained to him, "are what's inside of them, though sometimes they don't look much like that. I think these people tried to make things always look better than they really were."

Alovar nodded, still in awe of the treasure.

She led him away to another room where she had spread a sleeping mat across the floor. In this chamber was a small fire pit set in the center. Katherine explained that the smoke was vented out through pipes set in the ceiling. The smoke came to the surface three buildings away. It was almost impossible for anyone to ever locate her. Then she showed him the candles she had found and how she would light them at night.

Alovar paced around the room, examining every piece of it, surprised to find something like this so safe and secure in this wreck of a city. It had never occurred to him to try to actually live inside one of the buildings. He had always feared their creakings and the destroyed look of them.

"How long have you lived here?" he asked, turning away from a drawing of some kind of fish on the wall.

"Since everyone went away," Katherine answered, and Alovar looked at her sharply. She had not spoken of this since that evening at the campfire.

"How long ago was that?" he asked, watching her closely.

She met his gaze. "Almost three seasons now."

"The Marauders?" he asked.

"Yes," she nodded, "the Marauders. They came, killing my mother and brother."

"And you?" he asked a moment later.

She turned away, shaking her head. "They did not kill me."

Alovar nodded, understanding that sometimes there are worse things.

"And you have lived all this time alone?"

"Yes," she said, turning back to him. "Why do you seem surprised? Haven't you done the same?"

"I have."

"Then you should understand."

"Understand what?" Alovar said.

"This," Katherine said, reaching out to take his hand to lead him to the mirror. Together they stood in front of it, looking at their images. Both of them admiring the other until their eyes met and they turned to see what the other was seeing. Their bodies amazed them. Their unblemished faces, unlined by time or hardship, looked back at them.

Alovar stared at his image, then watched as the other reflection standing beside him slowly lifted her hand and placed it in his. He watched the reflections join their hands, then slowly turn to each other.

In the ancient city, in the center of the burnt lands, beyond all civilized society, Alovar found a sense of peace. For the first time in his life he had something more than his sword that brought him a sense of his own life. He almost felt safe.

At first this frightened him. It was so foreign. He didn't trust it and thought it might be some kind of trap. But as the days passed, he was unable to doubt its probity any longer. He gave himself to it, and found in this an answering gift from the woman he held.

Alovar moved to her underground room. They spent their days wandering the city, discovering treasures and mysteries from the past and their nights discovering the mysteries in each other, so long withheld from even themselves.

Alovar would occasionally awake in the middle of the night, his hand flashing toward his sword, unable to believe in the silence and the warmth around him. His hand would fumble along the body beside him, waking her. And Katherine would turn to him and, holding him, still his fear.

He in turn would offer the same solace for the demons that plagued her dreams, holding her until the perspiration dried on her body and the chills had passed. In the morning neither of them would speak of these visions, they would ignore them, occasionally glancing at the other when they thought they would not be observed.

Their eyes traced the other's features, finding a resonance of the perfection they saw in their own. It was a source of belonging that neither of them had ever thought possible.

Alovar went alone to the building that towered far above the ancient city. He climbed its many steps quickly and pushed through the last door without hesitation, having long since overcome his fear.

He approached the edge and looked out towards the Realm, seeing it as a distant smudge against the arid sand. He stared at it, thinking of what it was and what he had always mistakenly considered it to be. He thought of Staron and Staron's last words to him, and now found he had the words with which to reply.

He had begun to feel that maybe Katherine's way was wrong as well, that maybe their appearance was not a curse, to be reviled, but a way to light the path. He found himself thinking about the paper books and how the people who smiled within their pages were not like them at all. Those people were destroyers and seemed to take enjoyment in their destructions. This was not his way and had never been. He had battled often but never for the joy of it. That lust was not his but it was a hunger he had seen in the Marauders and in those in the Realm. Only the mutants, Alovar decided, seemed to be free of this desire. It was only they who accepted what came and who offered little struggle against it. And it was they that Alovar had found himself defending since his banishment.

He wondered if these things he had learned could be shared. Would there be anyone in the Realm who would listen to him? Would Staron listen, he wondered, remembering the heavy words of the man and the sadness with which they had been said. How much did Staron understand and how much could Staron accept? Could he accept a truth that would forever change the Realm, or was his only concern the Realm itself, regardless of the destruction this caused everyone else? Alovar did not know, but standing there, he decided he would have to find out.

He would speak to Katherine. As he turned from the edge, he saw a puff of dust far off to the east. He stared, watched it grow larger, then quickly rushed to the door and down the stairs.

He went swiftly through the ancient city to Katherine's camp. He burst down the steps to the underground room, calling her name. He stopped in the center of the room, hearing only the silence answer him. For a moment he caught a glimpse of himself in the mirror and was surprised by the savagery he saw reflected. He turned away and rushed up the steps.

He went through the city calling out to her. He went unrewarded. At the eastern edge of the city, he stared out across the sand. Now he could make out the figures of those approaching. Three were men on horses and another six ran along beside them. From the saddle of one of the horses rose a banner. On the white bit of cloth was drawn a sword descending on a skull. The sword's edge was etched in blood. It was a banner that Alovar had seen often before and had grown to hate. Marauders.

He watched them approach and rushed back through the city, calling again for Katherine. She never answered. He knew that she must be exploring another of the underground rooms, and could think of no way to warn her. He counted on her ability to survive and hid himself in the room they had come to inhabit together.

He crouched in a corner of the room with the grate above his head, straining his ears to hear the progress of the Marauders. He kept thinking about Katherine, assuring himself of her prowess, remembering the way she had been before he had met her, the ease with which she moved through the ruins and her remarks about the Marauders, how they feared the place.

He silently listened. He could hear the Marauders' raucous shouts and laughter. Their voices grew quiet as they rode into the streets. Alovar strained to hear them.

"It is evil," he heard one of them say, and agreed and wished that they would leave.

"It is only dead," said another. "And what is death to us, but food." He laughed, and was joined by the others.

Alovar heard their fear beneath the laughter and hoped that they would soon discover this as well.

They dismounted a few buildings away. He heard the creak of leather and the sharp sounds of their swords slapping against their belts. He listened closely and was dismayed when he heard the sound of wood and debris being broken. They were preparing a fire.

Alovar listened to them, watching the sun slowly fade from his room. As the time wore on, he felt sure that Katherine was aware of them, or else she would have appeared by now. Realizing this, he felt more secure about her.

Night came. Alovar could make out the dim light of their fire through his grate. One of them walked right above him. Alovar cowered below, but the man never glanced down, and even if he had, Alovar assured himself, he would have seen only darkness.

The night dragged on. Alovar remained vigilant, thinking about Katherine, finding his memories of her much sharper than ever before. He recalled his earlier decision to go back to the Realm to try to convince them of the truth. He now disdained this decision. What did it matter what they thought? He would live his life here with Katherine and leave the world outside the boundaries of their city. If any came to join them, fine, but he would not seek them out. Here he had found an oasis. Was it right for any man to expect anything more? A man was only what he could hold and protect. To seek out more than this, more than what he needed, was only to fall into the trap of the ancient ones, with their surface beauty that barely hid the ugliness beneath.

Alovar watched the morning slowly crawl across his room. He heard the Marauders waken and start their morning fire, and hoped that they would leave now.

"That building. There, see what it has," he heard one of them order, and stood, trying to peer through the grate to discover what building they had named.

He heard them approach and stepped away from the grate. They stopped at the edge of the structure above him, and Alovar knew what building they intended to search. He felt secure in his underground room, knowing the impossibility of discovery.

"There are footprints," he heard one of the men call above, and then heard the sound of other feet rushing to join those who stood above him.

"They are old."

"How old?"

"Old enough so that those who made them are bones," one said, and the others laughed.

"Look, they lead this way."

Alovar followed their sounds to the inside of his building. His hand fell to his sword and he moved quietly to the door, preparing himself for discovery. Even their discovery of his prints would not enable them to figure out the workings of the trap door, except by accident. But he prepared himself just the same.

He stepped to the side and waited, hearing them right above him. They were muttering angrily, unable to discover where the footprints led.

"They disappear," one said in awe.

"Bah! How can that be possible?"

"They do. Look at how they end at this wall."

He heard more of them enter to examine this mystery.

Later when he thought of this, he realized it was their sudden rush into the building that caused her to believe he had been discovered. He also realized that, when she rushed inside, she must have expected him to be there to help her. He wondered what she had thought when she charged inside to see only the Marauders. And when he pictured this, he would scream, knowing what she had thought, hating her for having done this thing to him.

He was not aware that she was there until he heard one of the men above him shout. "What the—" was all he managed before he fell. Alovar heard his thumping across the door above and then her shrill scream as she rushed among them.

Alovar darted towards the door, drawing his sword. He heard bodies fall across the door above him. He scaled the ladder and jammed his shoulder into it. It wouldn't budge. He strained against it, screaming, as the muscles of his back and shoulders threatened to burst. He stepped back and threw himself at the door. Still it wouldn't move.

He heard the struggle going on above him, powerless to do

anything but listen. He attacked the door with his sword, but the metal spit his sword back at him, dulling its edge.

He heard the men above him, grunting with their effort, trying to contain her. Suddenly the bodies shifted away from the door and he prepared himself to attack it again. Then he heard a yelp of pain and knew it was Katherine. He heard the sound of a body falling across the door. He hurled himself once more at it. At the last moment before he hit it, he heard the thump of a knife being jammed into wood above him. It was her knife, her last effort had been to try to save him. Her knife blocked the entranceway of the door, locking him inside, insuring his safety.

He battered himself against the door, throwing himself at it again and again, falling back to the floor each time. Blood flowed from his forehead and eye, blinding him.

He heard them above him. He heard their grunting and exhulutions of breath as they dragged her out of the building. He threw himself at the door, one last effort, using every bit of strength. But it did not yield. It flung him back onto the floor in a daze. He lay there, trying to regain consciousness, listening to the slobbering of the men above him. He saw them briefly against the grate, then saw her thrown across it, stripped of clothes.

"My pretty one," he heard one of them growl, then heard another laugh obscenely. "She's perfect, not a blemish on her," he heard, then heard her scream once, and then grow quiet as the men used her, then used her again.

Alovar battered his head against the floor, cursing them, her, and himself for ever thinking they would be safe here.

The noises seemed to go on forever above him. The slapping of flesh, the heavy panting of the men, her silence.

In the end he hid himself in her silence. He took it into himself and held it like a child, deep to his breast, until it grew into something that was so monstrous that it knew no name.

"What do we do with her?"

"Cover her. We'll take her with us to keep us warm by the fire."
One of them laughed.

Alovar waited. He heard them laughing, yawning in exhaustion.
He heard one of them move across the floor. He rose silently and
approached the door. He caught a glimpse of himself in the mirror
and paused for a moment, unable to recognize this image. Blood
had dried across his face and his features were frozen into a look of
utterly cold perfection. It was a face from the pages of the paper
books.

He stepped to the door and waited . . .

He heard someone grab the knife, then heard the screech of it as
it was withdrawn from the entranceway of the door. He reached up
and pushed. The door opened easily, and Alovar moved through.

He caught the first man at the edge of the building and
wrenched his head back; then Alovar drew his sword across the
enemy's neck. The wound showered two others in blood. In a flash
Alovar moved among them, swinging his sword like a scythe, willing
it to bite deep into their bodies.

He moved towards the others, bathed in blood, his eyes impassive, seeing nothing before him but death. *Whose* death made little
difference.

He glanced towards the woman's body lying across the grate,
and saw only that, just a body, nothing more.

He lifted his sword as two of the Marauders charged him. He
deflected one of the blows and felt the other's sword cut into his left
arm. The pain fed him. He hungered for more as he lifted his sword
and brought it flashing across the other's neck. The head toppled
from its shoulders, spouting blood in a huge carnelian fountain.
Alovar laughed and moved towards the other one as two more
stepped forward to join their companion.

His sword flashed in the hazy sunlight, wielded by something that was no longer human, by something that had crawled from the bowels of the earth transformed.

He walked among them without hesitation. His sword slashing with such speed that it was only glimpsed as a blur of light. It cut and sawed its way through limbs, dashing bodies into crumpled heaps across the earth, until the sound of blood dripping into the sand was all that remained in the silence.

Alovar stood, his sword to his side, and turned towards Katherine. He heard a groan to his right and lashed downwards, stilling the offending voice.

He gathered her in his arms and held her, not sure what to do. Her body was covered with scratches and bites. Her breasts were bared and smeared with dirt and sand. He wrapped her carefully in his tunic and carried her down below to their shelter.

He bathed her gently and laid her out beside him and held her throughout the day. He listened to the sound of her breathing and found it all he could hear. It echoed through him, and as much as he fought it, he found hope in its rhythmic exhalations.

The first night she lay without speaking.

The second day she opened her eyes in fear. For a moment she didn't recognize him and fought him. He held her until she quieted in his arms and seemed to sleep.

The third day he tried to force her to eat. But she slept and the food grew cold, ignored.

The fourth day she woke and seemed to recognize him. She smiled and reached into her robe. Alovar felt a burst of hope. She withdrew her hand and held it out to him. She opened her fist and into his hand dropped a ring still warm from her body. He glanced at it, then back at her. Her eyes glazed and slowly closed.

He bowed over her anxiously, putting his head to her chest, and was reassured to hear the sound of her heart. He held her tightly, rubbing her body, trying to bring her back. He called her name. Then, when he grew hoarse, whispered it, until finally the only sound was the ragged exhalation of his breath, each time ending with her name twisted silently on his lips.

On the fifth day . . .

CHAPTER
17

ON MY PORCH, coffee and cigarette in hand, I think about William Butler Yeats, or at least a line by him that seems to be in my mind. *Things fall apart; the centre cannot hold; Mere anarchy is loosed upon the world.*

Not a particularly pleasant line to wake up to, and I'm beginning to find the contemplation of it mildly depressing. It's that kind of morning. I slouch back against the wall and rub my spine, wondering where everyone went.

No one came up to see me yesterday. At the least I had expected the old woman to make an appearance, and at the most I had thought I would see Katherine. Neither of them showed. It disturbs me when I begin to think of possible reasons for this. Could the old woman be right? Is there that much to worry about? She knows more about these things than I do, but still, are people that curious, that intent on dissecting every little move and thought of those they know and don't know? It's not something I would have thought likely.

I take a last drag of my cigarette and crush it out beneath my foot, thinking, Bah, the old woman's always been a pessimist.

I rise, yawn hugely, and think about gathering wood. This holds little appeal. I decide that I'll do twice as much tomorrow. I go into the cabin and return to the porch with Alovar and three Oreo cookies. I munch away, trying not to drool on Alovar, and work on my notes for the next chapter.

I reread what I've done so far and decide that I can't kill off Katherine. It depresses me too much to even consider doing this. Having her attacked and raped sent me into a rage that took me hours to recover from. Killing her off, I have a feeling, would be infinitely worse.

I toy with various endings for Alovar and Katherine but can't seem to come up with anything. Nothing seems to ring true.

I glance up sharply, hearing a distant vehicle but it passes far below me on the highway. I listen to it retreat, wondering where my Katherine was yesterday. It doesn't take much thought for me to come up with a possible answer.

I know the old woman must have talked to her. What she said I cannot even imagine. I trust Katherine enough to know that she would speak to me first before she decided anything. Thinking this, my hand drifts to the ring hanging from my neck. I hold it for a moment, then bring it up to my nostrils, sniffing it noisily until I pick up a vague memory of her scent. The odor floods my sinuses and works its way into my brain.

For lunch I eat a couple cans of sardines, half a loaf of bread, and wash it all down with a beer. I burp, loudly, then step out into the front yard. I crouch over, examining the ground by the side of my cabin, looking for any trace of tulip tops. Katherine's told me nothing will happen for another couple of months, but I can't keep myself from examining the flower beds each day, just in case one decides to make an early appearance.

I find something green popping out of the earth at the far end on the east side of the cabin. I hunker down, squinting to examine it. I snort a moment later and pluck the offending caterpillar out of the earth. I throw it towards some bushes off to the side, growling at it, warning it not to try trespassing again or there will be worse coming its way.

I fumble around the cabin, doing odd chores that don't really need to be done but occupy me enough to keep my mind off Katherine.

Where is she? She's never missed two days in a row. And where is the old woman? After seeing her the other day, I could tell that she wasn't going to leave this alone. I fully expected to see her yesterday, and if not then, certainly today. What's happened to her? Maybe it's her knee, I decide, remembering it again, remembering the way he stood above us, the flash of the ax. I growl beneath my breath, startling a butterfly, and watch it fly into the forest.

I cock my ears towards the path but hear only silence and the stirring of a rabbit. I dash off into the woods, trying to lose my thoughts in its verdancy.

Through the trees I race, arms outstretched above my head, jaws gnashing the wind, occasionally dropping to all fours to navigate around an obtruding bush or duck a limb.

At the foot of the mountain, I stretch out on my side and roll in the brush, feeling the dirt on the floor of the forest cover my finely combed hair and begin to mat it. I don't care. I have already decided that I will be left alone again today. I growl at the thought, then lying on my side light a cigarette and watch the way the smoke rises before my eyes. I snap at it playfully, then standing, lean back against a ledge and look up at the peaks above me. I think about climbing the mountain again, about rising to its top and howling until my lungs are filled and cleaned with the thin air. But I stub out my cigarette instead, deciding that it would take more energy than I have at the moment.

I race down to the stream and watch the trout float along its bottom, darting to the surface to snap at flies and water spiders. Watching them feed makes me hungry. I take my time going back to the cabin, listening to the forest around me, hearing squirrel, rabbit, and the shriek of a fox. I long to join in with their cries but know mine would only frighten theirs away. I walk home silently, wondering what's happened to Katherine, to the old woman.

In the evening I work on Alovar again, forcing myself not to do anything to Alovar's Katherine. I'm in an irritable mood and find myself wanting to commit more mayhem upon her. I can't believe she didn't come up today. I hold her ring for a moment, thinking about the way Alovar had so recently held his, and I wonder if I shouldn't rewrite that last chapter. Maybe I shouldn't have done that to his Katherine, but at the same time I find myself so annoyed with my Katherine that I somewhat crazily find myself thinking she deserved it.

I turn on the radio, flicking from channel to channel until I find a song by Laibach. I start dancing, slowly at first, but then, as the music takes me, I give myself over to it until soon I'm prancing around the room like a whirlwind. My teeth gnash the air as I jump up, slapping the beams in time with the beat. Arms flapping in front of me, legs darting out left and right, the scrape of nails on the floor — I dance wildly until I'm exhausted and crawl over on all fours to flip off the radio.

I lie on my side in a heap, gasping for breath. From my vantage point I can look out through the open curtain at the moon. It glimmers hugely in the thin mountain air. I lie quietly, watching it slowly rise. I try not to think of Katherine as I hold her ring tightly, using it as a talisman to ward off her image.

When I sleep, I dream of my house. It's the same as always: the TV, the sound of neighbors, the sense of belonging. Then the knock at the door. I rise, not knowing who will be there. I answer the door and it's Katherine, smiling at me. She steps inside and hugs me. I feel her arms close around me and her hands clasp my back, pressing my body against hers. I feel the full length of her against me, the absolute warmth of another human being. And it's so real it wakes me, and as I wake, I'm vaguely ashamed to find each of my eyes leaking lugubriously down my hairy cheeks. I wipe them, then flip over on my other side and sleep again, this time dreamlessly.

I wake and rush outside to shower, noticing the frost splayed out across the forest in a icy pane of sparkling light.

Shivering, I dart back inside and begin breakfast. I eat, then carry my coffee and cigarette out to the front porch. I examine my tulips, wondering how they're doing under all that cold dirt, then dress and go off to gather wood.

I take down an old hickory tree and drag it to the back of the cabin. I spend most of the morning cutting and splitting it, occasionally stopping to sniff the air. Fall is over, I decide, winter has come. I glance out at the trees, almost bare now, and see the grotesque postures of their unclothed limbs twisting into the air. I swing the ax, thinking how much better they look with their clothes on.

I shower again and carefully comb myself until every hair is neatly in place except for the ones I can't quite reach on my back. These I flatten down by mashing myself against the wall of the cabin. When I'm satisfied that I'm neatly groomed, I step out onto the porch to wait. I know she'll come today. Two days are excusable. Three would be something else, I think, nervously lighting a cigarette as I snort the wind, wondering what to do if she doesn't appear.

Two hours later I hear the unmistakable sound of her car. I yelp, leaping off the porch, having just about given up on her. She's never been this late before.

I race down the path, then dart off into the brush and wait. I pick off a few burrs and smooth down my hair as I peer out anxiously towards the gate.

A few moments later her yellow Volkswagen appears, I have to hug myself to stop from howling.

She climbs out of her car, wearing her frayed jeans and the white embroidered blouse. My favorites, I think, watching her intently.

She stoops down and pulls out a blue windbreaker and puts it on. I can't help myself from growling softly.

She opens the gate, then steps inside without locking it. I look at her curiously, wondering what this means.

"Are you there?" she calls.

I pull my gaze from the gate to her. "Yes."

"I can't stay."

The words come at me like blows. I seem to feel each of them punch into my chest until it's difficult to breathe.

"Why?" I ask, trying unsuccessfully to keep the dismay from my voice.

"Don't sound like that. It's not up to me."

"Then who's it up to?"

She shakes her head and turns away, looking back at her car.

I watch her closely, sensing something, not sure what. I sniff the air noisily, drawing in her scent. I pull it deep into my nostrils and hold it there, examining it closely. It's all hers but today there's something different. I'm not quite sure what. It's something that I know but am unable to name, at least unable to name in relation to Katherine.

"Things have happened," she says, without turning.

I snort hugely, pulling in her scent again. I examine it, pushing away the soap, the perfume, the piquant odor of her sweat, until all I'm left with is the one vague disquieting aroma I've smelled before.

"What?" I force myself to ask, sniffing more of this odor, trying to find its source, too afraid to think the obvious one.

"Things," she answers, turning to look fully towards my hiding place.

"What things?" I ask again, then can't help myself from asking, "Why are you afraid?"

I'm ashamed of the question, but am more afraid of her answer. I wished I'd never asked it as I watch her try to think how to answer.

She glances away, then looks back and says unsteadily, "Your mother."

"Yes?"

"She's ill."

"Yes, I know. I saw her the other day. Her leg is bothering her again," I say, thinking, please, go on, tell me what the trouble is, let's not bicker about the old woman.

Katherine shakes her head, and I suddenly realize what she's saying.

"What, what is it?" I growl.

Katherine steps back, hearing the violence in my voice.

For a moment I feel a small dash of shame, but it quickly disappears when I think of what she's just said.

"Tell me," I demand, gripping the trunk of the tree in front of me and squeezing it.

"She's had a stroke," Katherine says quickly, rushing the words together, trying to get them out so quickly that their effect will be lessened.

The words shock me. I can't understand them. How could this happen to her? Admittedly she's old, but she's not that old. There must be some mistake, I think, looking up at Katherine, who still stands near the gate staring into the woods.

"I can't stay," she says. "I have to get back. There's too many things going on right now."

"What, what could be going on now?" I ask, thinking of the old woman, thinking how everything must surely stop while this poor old woman recovers and grows back to health.

"Things," Katherine answers vaguely, shaking her head.

"What *things?*" I yell, startling a flock of birds from a nearby tree. They screech in annoyance as they take flight.

"Edward," Katherine says patiently, "I'd like to stay with you, but it's dangerous right now. Between your mother and my uncle, things have gotten very weird in town."

I listen to this, smelling the underlying odor of her body, and realize that she's lying to me. I want to howl and to rush out and grab her until she tells me the truth, but all I feel is a heavy sense of weariness.

"Go then," I tell her.

She reaches into her windbreaker and pulls out a small blue notebook. She places it on the gatepost and says, "This is your mother's diary. I think you should read it."

"Go away," I tell her, finding her voice painful, thinking

it promises so much but seems to give so little, just like all the other voices I've ever heard in my life.

"Edward, please, try to understand. It's not that I want to leave you, it's because I have to. My uncle's crazy right now. He talked to that guy who saw my car up here. He thinks I'm seeing someone up here. He thinks—"

I interrupt her: "And aren't you? Aren't you seeing me?"

"Yes, but it's not like that. He wouldn't understand. He's half crazy with worry about your mother, and it's like he's focusing everything on me right now. I had to sneak out of the window just to come up here."

"Why are you afraid?" I blurt out.

"What? What'd you mean?" she asks, taking a step back, one hand rising to her forehead.

"I can smell it on you," I snarl, hating the sound of my own voice but unable to stop it. I find a small visceral part of me enjoying the act of causing her pain, and even as I realize that this pain is only a reflection of my own, I still can't stop it.

"That's not fair. I am afraid. But I'm afraid for you."

"Maybe of me," I say.

She shakes her head. "You're only doing this because you're hurt. It's not me, it's your mother, Edward, and she's very sick. Can't you at least admit that to yourself?"

I howl. I can't stop myself. It bursts out of my chest before I even know it's there.

I see her step back, but still can't help myself.

"Admit *what?*" I demand. "That that blowsy old woman could possibly mean anything to me? Look at what she's done to me, look at what she's *made* me!" I scream.

Katherine raises her head and glares at my hiding place, "*You son of a bitch!*" she yells. "You blame her for what you are.

What the *hell* right do you have to do that? She carted you around from one end of the country to the other. She never had to do that. She killed her husband for you, for Christ's sake. What the fuck *more* do you want from her?"

Her words steal my own. For a moment there's only the wind in the trees around us.

"She told you," I finally say meekly.

"Yes . . . and more," Katherine answers.

I cringe from her tone and suddenly it all seems to fall in around me. I think of the Yeats line and feel the center slowly breaking apart.

I howl and dart off into the woods, back towards the cabin. I run as I've never run before, losing myself in the motion, letting my body become my brain until its actions are the only thought I know. My howl trails behind me, echoing off the trees, sending birds shrieking into the air.

Inside the cabin I cower beside my bed, flanks heaving, trying to draw in huge gulps of oxygen, eyes leaking into the fine mat of hair on my cheeks, until it runs and drips from the whiskers on each side of my jaw. I crouch there, thinking of a world without a center.

I listen to the sound of my breathing. The only intrusion on the silence around me. I hear each gasp and hoarse breath rattle through my throat, thinking that this is enough. I will lie here until I slowly die and decay into dust. Years from now some hiker will come across the cabin and admire the tulips and the clean stacks of wood that bracket my home, never having the faintest idea what lived here, what manner of beast inhabited this bucolic idyll.

I hear her voice before I'm aware she's out there. I become aware of it, sensing that it's been going on for a while, but its rhythms are so like the gasps from my lungs that I haven't noticed it before.

" 'He's my son, and sometimes I wish that I could take it all away from him. I wish that I could give him half of what he has given me,' " I hear her say, and I rise dizzily and listen.

" 'He came out today and showed me the stream he found back in the woods. Watching him, I was reminded of when he was a little boy, of how excited he used to get over the littlest thing, things that I'd never even noticed before. Watching him then, and today, made me feel like I was a young girl again, seeing it all over for the first time.' "

I stumble towards the window.

" 'I know it's not right for me to feel this way, but when I hold him, when he lets me, which isn't too often now, I feel so good, as if we're a family again and everything'll always be all right as long as we have each other.' "

I lean towards the window and part the curtain.

" 'Eddie told me today that he forgives his father. He said he understood him and doesn't hold it against him what he did. I couldn't look at him. I couldn't tell him how ashamed I was that I couldn't do the same.' "

I look out at Katherine holding the small book in her hand, turning the pages, then pausing and reading.

" 'He won't come out to see me. He won't hardly talk to me anymore. I don't know what to do. I try to apologize to him, but he doesn't listen. I guess it's what I deserve, but it hurts so much knowing how much I hurt him.' "

She reads on: " 'Went up again today to see Eddie. He wouldn't come out. I left the food on his doorstep and went back up the path. I hid behind some juniper bushes and watched him come out to get them. It was good seeing him again. He looks like he's taken care of himself. I wonder if he ever thinks about me up there. Does he know what he's doing? How this makes me feel?'"

I lean my forehead against the sill and close my eyes.

"'And when he stood that way, I couldn't help myself from putting my arms around him. Holding him, all I could feel was the warmth of him.'"

She closed the book and looked up at the cabin.

"This is your mother, Edward. This isn't some old woman who just happens to cart up groceries for you."

"I know," I answer weakly.

"Say it."

I can't.

"Say it," she demands again.

"Mother," I say softly, and feel my eyes cloud. After a moment I ask, "How is she, Katherine?"

"Not good."

"Will she—" I start, stop, then go on again. "Will she be all right?" I ask instead.

"They think so, but she'll never be the same. It took the left side of her body, Edward. She's paralyzed."

I groan and bang my head against the wall.

"I wasn't afraid of you. I was afraid for you," she says quietly. "You can't believe everything you see, and you can't always believe everything you think."

How can I answer?

"I have to go. I don't know what my uncle will do."

I nod, sniffle, and push myself away from the wall.

"Will you walk me down?" she asks, and I bare my teeth gently, thinking how far I would be willing to walk with her, and how impossible a walk it would be.

"Yes."

I watch her start up the path, and before she's halfway up I step outside the door and pick up the blue book on the porch. I carry it back inside and place it on my desk, then go out the door and into the woods.

"Are you there?" she calls.

"Yes."

"She told me to tell you not to worry."

"How?" I almost groan.

"It was the first thing she said."

I pause to lean against a birch tree. I close my eyes, feeling the papery bark scrape against my hair.

"Do you want me to . . ." Katherine starts to say, but I push myself away from the tree and answer before she completes the question:

"Tell my mother not to worry about me. Tell her to just take care of herself, that's all that matters right now. I'll be fine and I'll be thinking of her."

Katherine pauses and smiles.

I reach up to touch the ring hanging from around my neck.

Near the foot of the gate Katherine pauses again. I watch her from behind a holly bush.

"I want you to do something for me, Edward," she says quietly, looking out at the woods.

"Yes?"

"I want you to come out."

"No!"

"I know about you now."

"The old—" I start to say, then stop myself. "My mother?" I ask.

"Yes, she told me. She thought I didn't understand."

"You don't."

"If I don't, then who ever will?" she says, her arms at her sides as she calmly watches the woods, waiting for me to appear.

I can't, I think, then touch the ring around my neck and think, how can I not?

"Turn around," I tell her, and wait for her to do this.

I brush the leaves as well as I can from my body. I push back my ears, feeling them pop right back up, then take a small step out from behind the bush.

She stands in the middle of the path, staring off to the side.

I step out from behind the bush. The weeds cover my legs to the knees. For the first time in my life my body is in full view of another person, a stranger. It makes me feel naked and afraid. I take a step back behind the bush.

"Please, Edward," she says, and her voice stops my retreat.

I force myself to step through the weeds to the path until I'm only ten feet from her.

"Don't turn just yet," I tell her, then go on nervously. "I'm ugly, Katherine. My body is beyond anything you can . . . It will repulse you."

"It might," she agrees.

"Then why do this?"

"Because I don't think it will. Because I think you're more than what you might look like, and I trust your mother, Edward. If she could love you as much as she does, how could you be anything else but beautiful?"

I can't answer her. There are no words left to explain me.

"I'm going to turn now, Edward," Katherine says, and begins to move.

I try to watch her, but can't. My eyes fall to the ground and to my feet. I see the stubby toes, the sharp elongated nails extended and digging into the earth, and wait for her to scream.

I sense her turn, then feel her eyes on me. I wait, expecting a sound, some semblance of shock, but hear only the steadiness of her breath entering and leaving her lungs. I slowly raise my head to meet her gaze straight on, waiting for the look I know will be there.

What I see instead is a smile, Katherine's smile. "You're wearing it," is what she says.

I glance down, following her gaze to my chest and to the ring that lies there, sparkling beneath the sunlight in my hair and look back up at her.

"You *are* ugly, Edward. There's no denying that," she says, and I grin, baring my teeth at her.

She takes a step towards me, and I see her more closely than I have ever seen her before. I see every line of her face and the color of her eyes, and her scent washes over me like a mountain stream until all that's left is her, standing in front of me, hesitantly reaching out to touch my arm. The warmth of her hand burns its way through me, until it's a touch that will never again be forgotten.

"Edward," she says, smiling at me, touching me, looking up at me in awe. "You're beautiful."

And I grin at her hugely, baring teeth that have never before been seen, helpless to stop the smile.

She reaches up to touch the ring around my neck, then reaches further to touch my cheek.

I press my face against her hand and reach out to touch her, to actually feel her flesh beneath my own.

"Kat, get away from it!"

For a moment the shout freezes us like a picture. I'm

unable to move. I'm locked in the moment before — smiling, reaching for her.

"*Kat, move away,*" comes the shout again.

I move, whirling back a step, crouching, baring my teeth towards the sound and snorting the air. I smell the men and curse my stupidity in not being more aware of them. I also smell the oil of guns and search the woods by the gate.

A man steps out onto the path, leveling a rifle in my direction. I snarl, stepping back.

"No!" Katherine screams.

She reaches out behind her, touches my waist.

"No!" she cries, as I see two other men emerge from the woods, both carrying rifles.

I growl and find myself thinking of Alovar, of his impotence in the face of this same danger. I won't let it happen to Katherine.

I step in front of her, my teeth bared. A growl begins in my chest and escapes from my jaws. I move towards the men.

Katherine grabs me, wrenches me backwards. I stumble and hear a shot and then a curse coming from the woods.

I feel the rage welling up inside of me. I whirl around. Katherine's hands fall away from me; the anger is drowning me. I let it take me down and move towards them, becoming what I've always been perceived to be. I welcome it this time.

The man to my right lifts his rifle. I turn, face him, and roar. My voice shatters the mountainside. Fear climbs into his eyes and I smile, baring my teeth at him. Katherine calls out to me, but all I can see or smell are the men before me, their guns and their eyes trying to pierce my body. How easily their flesh will tear in my hands and jaws.

I scream at the man with the gun and start for him.

He shoulders his rifle. I grin even wider, welcoming the

challenge, my teeth biting into my lip. I let the pain hold me and move me forward.

Kathcrine calls out. Her voice stops me. I glance back at her over my shoulder. Her eyes quickly fall away, but in that instant I see everything. It's not these men and their perceptions that have made me what I am, it's me. It is my own belief in my monstrosity that has exiled me to these woods.

I throw my head back and scream.

"Edward," Katherine calls. "Please, Edward."

She holds her arms out to me.

I move towards her.

"Get away from it, Kat!" someone screams behind me.

"Edward," Katherine says, thcn smiles.

"Kat!" one of the men screams again.

I hear the shot, feel the snap of the bullet as it passes by me. I still the growl that starts in my chest and lift my hands, holding them palm outward, surrendering, thinking it is time to end this.

I step towards the men, see their eyes, see the horror, and then I smell blood. I turn. Katherine is sprawled on the path, blood soaking through the front of her shirt. I howl at the top of my lungs. The sound freezes the men. I crouch beside her.

"It hurts," she says, then reaches up to gently touch my face. "Run, Edward," she tells me. When I make no move to leave her, she winces. "Please, I'll be all right."

A burly man raises his weapon. I lunge backwards in a whirl of dust and weeds and dart into the woods.

I circle and come up on the side of them, watching the men race forward to crouch over Katherine, who lies silently in the center of the path. I want to charge across the weeds and dismember them. I want to be Alovaric in my rage, but I force myself to wait and listen.

"She'll be all right," one of them says, and then he stoops and picks her up in his arms.

How I envy him those arms, those two normal-looking twigs that so easily lift her to his chest.

"What about that thing?" one of them asks, and the other, the one carrying Katherine, turns his head and spits out, "Kill it."

I watch Katherine disappear into her car. My last sight of her is of her hair, the yellow streak running like a great divide down her scalp.

The men step off the path as the car starts down the hill. I turn and race off into the woods towards Flag Mountain. Reaching its foot, I hug the rock to my chest and climb. My hands and feet begin to bleed and I leave trails of blood smeared across the rock.

I approach the peak, wheezing, thinking Katherine was right, cigarettes have taken their toll.

I launch myself up and out, to claw at the ledge sloping up to the ridge. I grip it and swing my body up and over, using my feet and nails to propel me to the safety of the lip, then lie there panting, staring down at the forest below. It looks far away and peaceful. Are the hunters searching through my cabin? What will they think of the things they find? Can they read? Maybe one of them has even read my books. What would he think if he learned that what he hunts is what has amused him? In the evenings, by the warmth of his fire, with the sound of his children upstairs and the comfortable drone of the TV before him, could he have sat reading one of my books? Would he care, I wonder.

They hunt because that is what they do, I decide, giving myself up to Alovar and his awareness.

I dangle my legs over the edge and light a cigarette. I have three left after this one, and decide that I will smoke all of them before I do anything else.

I smoke, pausing to snuff the wind, picking up the scent of deer and squirrel. I inhale their gamey odor and hold it until it disappears beneath another puff from my cigarette.

Once I lift my nose to the wind, sure that I've picked up the scent of a bear. But the scent is too distant to identify with certainty. I wonder what a bear would do, coming in contact with something like me. Would he come to me as a friend, or would he think of me as only a part of the society that threatens him? I would confuse him, I decide, looking like one thing but smelling like another. It would be a reaction that would certainly be justified. At least *he* would give me the benefit of sight as well as scent, I think, somewhat wryly.

I finish off my second cigarette, trying not to let my thoughts go off in dangerous directions. Involuntarily my hand rises to the ring hung around my neck. I clasp it tightly, thinking of her smile, thinking of the way she smiled at *me* — actually seeing me and still being able to smile.

Her words, admitting my ugliness, causing no pain whatsoever, followed so closely by those other words, those words that I cannot believe. Those words that even now, sitting on this ridge, watching the world so far below, I could never possibly imagine anyone saying or thinking about me.

I howl. Ripping it out into the mountainous air. A hawk swoops away and moves off to another ridge to try to decide what manner of beast this is.

I light my last cigarette from the butt end of the other, then stand and move to the far side of the mountain. I stand at the edge, looking down at the forest below. It stretches for miles, unbroken by cabins or man, only a lake, a dim spot of blue, dots this vista. Far off I see the sun beginning to color a distant eastern peak as it starts to set. I watch the shadow slowly descend over its face, knowing that soon it will touch mine.

I shiver, suddenly chilled by the air. I snort, then inhale the scent of winter. It seems close and will soon cover everything beneath a blanket of white, smoothing out the awkward shapes and contours of the land until they blend into one smooth fabric of white.

My last cigarette burns below the halfway mark. I look at it fondly, thinking of the companionship it has offered me over the years. So neat in its appearance and disappearance. In many ways, I think, I will soon emulate it.

I drag deeply, then stub the butt out on the rock. My nails scratch the surface, leaving a thin trail of five claw marks. I crouch down for a moment to examine them, thinking that this is my mark. All else I have scrawled under other names, other identities, but this scratched trail, clawed into the rock, is my own. Will it ever be discovered? Then I rise and step to the edge of the summit.

I glance back one last time, thinking of the cabin, of Alovar, and how we both had desired the impossible. And then I turn and leap.

My howl echoing across the floor of the valley below announces my arrival, warning all who stand in my way that I am coming.

I bare my teeth, feeling the wind rush up to meet me and hold me in its uneasy embrace.

CHAPTER
18

ON THE FIFTH day, she died.

Alovar carried her from the underground room to the surface of the world. He walked through the decaying bodies of the marauders without seeing them.

He carried her to the edge of the ancient city and then up a sandy slope overlooking it. There he found the two mounds of rocks she had told him about.

He knelt down and, using his hands, began to dig.

He dug deep into the damaged earth, then stopped and knelt on his heels. His hands folded together and toyed with the ring he had slipped over his little finger.

He gently lifted her and placed her in the earth, then slowly covered her beneath the sand.

He carried stone from the city to mark her grave, and finally, as the sun hit the western horizon, he stood over the mound of sand, marked by the broken stone, and stared down at it.

Alovar stayed by her side until darkness fell around him, then he turned and walked slowly back into the city.

He camped on the surface, unable to face the prospect of ever entering the underground room again.

In the morning he climbed to the top of the tallest building and looked out over the burnt sands to the distance boundaries of the Realm.

He thought about what was there and what it meant. His hand rose to his face, tracing the smooth untouched flesh, and realized that flesh was nothing more than a curtain, hiding its occupant from the world.

It is time now, Alovar thought, to tear this curtain aside.

He descended the stairs, then walked across the floor of the ruined city until he stood beside her grave.

Perfection, Alovar thought, drawing his sword and offering it in salute to the woman beneath the sand, is only a matter of perception.

With this thought, he lifted the edge of the sword to his face and began to cut, to prepare himself to rejoin society and to show it the true face of civilization.

ABOUT THE AUTHOR

Jeff Collignon was born in Poughkeepsie, New York, and raised in Waukegan, Illinois, a small industrial suburb, northeast of Chicago. He left both Waukegan and school as soon as he was of legal age and took to the road. He has barely stopped moving since. In his thirty-eight years, he has lived in or passed through forty-eight states, Canada, Mexico and Europe.